W9-CBR-800

In the House of the Enemy

In the House of the Enemy

Bea Carlton

FIC
CAR
c.1 10/89

ACCENT BOOKS
Denver, Colorado

COCHISE COUNTY LIBRARY
DRAWER
ISLEE SAM

ACCENT BOOKS

A division of Accent Publications, Inc.
12100 W. Sixth Avenue
P.O. Box 15337
Denver, Colorado 80215

Copyright ©1983 Accent Publications, Inc.
Printed in the United States of America

All rights reserved. No portion of this book may be reproduced in any form
without the written permission of the publishers, with the exception of brief
excerpts in magazine reviews.

Library of Congress Catalog Number 83-073041

ISBN 0-89636-122-5

FIC CARLTON   c.1

Carlton, Bea.

In the house of the enemy

DATE DUE

NOV 18 1989		MAY 29 1990	
NOV 28 1989			
DEC 20 1989		JUN 13 1990	
JAN 4 1990		JUN 22 1990	
		AUG 9 1990	
FEB 1 1990		SEP 5 1990	
FEB 22 1990			
FEB 28 1990		SEP 14 1990	
APR 4 1990		OCT 31 1990	
APR 25 1990			

HAS CATALOG CARDS

DEMCO

3 9311 00056 9224

1

When he first saw her, Eric Ford was driving along at a leisurely rate just at the edge of town. She was walking rapidly toward him down the sundrenched sidewalk, ash-blond hair bouncing with each energetic step. Eric's eyes passed over her indifferently at first—then shock slammed into his stomach like an invisible fist, setting his heart to pounding and almost paralyzing his strong hands upon the wheel. A strangled mutter burst from his constricted throat, "It can't be Linn! It can't be! She's—dead!"

But the apparition had the same ash-blond hair, worn loose and parted in the middle above a pointed face; the same slender, long-limbed, neat figure; was about five feet, five inches tall and looked about twenty-three years old. It had to be her! But it couldn't be! Linn was dead—had been for three long years!

"Well, there's only one way to find out!"

The girl was well past now, and Eric was watching her rapid departure through the rearview mirror. His car nearly ran up on the curb. He quickly recovered it, parked hastily, and jumped out just as the figure turned the corner a block away.

Eric sprinted down the street, almost running down an indignant elderly matron and one slightly tipsy bar-patron who blundered into his path. He skidded to a walk just a step from the corner and rounded it at a fast clip. The girl was gone.

Eric surveyed the area with a quick glance. She would not have had time to reach the end of the block or cross the street. So she must have gone into one of the three doorways ahead, he speculated.

A few strides and he was looking in the window of the first shop—a small beauty parlor. Two women sat under hairdryers. One was turning the pages of a magazine idly, the other—a gum-chewing redhead—met his eyes briefly and looked away self-consciously. A manicurist was painstakingly doing the nails of a third, avidly-talking, customer. Eric scanned the interior but could see no one else.

Next was an insurance office. Eric opened the door and walked to the service counter. Two women worked there: one was elderly and plump, the other was young, pretty and brunette. A man, working at a large, cluttered desk, was the only other person in the main office. To the side and back were small partitioned cubicles. A low murmur of voices indicated the presence of people there.

"May I help you, sir?" the pretty brunette asked.

"Did my wife come in here?" inquired Eric. "She is blond and slender; she's wearing a green suit and carrying a shoulder-strap purse."

"Your wife didn't come in here but that sure fits the description of Dr. Glover's receptionist, next door." Dark eyes sparkled mischievously. "She just returned from lunch."

"Thanks," said Eric with a sheepish grin.

The next door bore the simple inscription—*Dr. Robert Glover, M.D.* Eric walked in. The girl was sitting at the reception desk, consulting an appointment book. Eric studied her intently. Had he inadvertently found Clay's wife? He would know in a minute. If this was Linn, she had green eyes and a tiny scar on the right side of her chin, on the jawline.

Eric strolled over casually and stood waiting before the desk. The girl wrote something in the book, then lifted her head and spoke in a crisp, professional voice.

"Did you wish to see the doctor?"

Eric searched her face for a quiet moment. A faint scar on the jawline clinched the identification but it was the eyes which captured his attention. He had forgotten how startlingly green they were, flecked with gold—expressive and arresting.

She stirred slightly under his scrutiny and spoke in a

louder voice. "Sir, did you wish to see the doctor?"

"No, I want to see you, Linn. Don't you remember me? You are Mrs. Linn Randolph, aren't you?"

The girl's face paled and she dropped her eyes as if in confusion; her slender fingers clinched and unclinched the open appointment book. Then she took a deep breath and tried to regain her professional demeanor, not quite succeeding.

"My name is Miss Linn Woods, not Mrs. Linn Randolph." She stretched out the slim, ringless fingers of her left hand, in an almost unconscious gesture. "Why—" Her voice quavered slightly, "Why did you call me Mrs. Linn Randolph?"

Eric regarded her gravely for a moment before he pulled out a wallet from his inside coat pocket, flipped it open to a picture, and dropped it onto the desk before the girl.

The picture was in color—a girl with shoulder-length ash-blond hair, green eyes, pointed chin with a barely discernible, tiny white scar; and next to the girl was a ruggedly handsome, dark-haired young man. Scrawled across the picture, near the bottom, were the words: "With love, Clay and Linn."

The girl picked up the picture with trembling fingers. "Where did you get this picture of me?"

Eric replied in a stern voice. "This is a picture Linn and Clay Randolph gave me about three years ago. Do you still deny you are Linn Randolph?"

The girl stared at him blankly for a moment. Suddenly she began to tremble. "Please—go—away," she said in a choked voice.

Reaching across the desk and gripping her shoulder, Eric shook her gently but urgently. "You are Linn Randolph, aren't you?"

"I don't know! I don't know!" the girl wailed.

Suddenly a curt masculine voice spoke, "What's going on here?"

Eric removed his hand quickly and saw the doctor

emerging from his office. He was a gentle-appearing, gray-haired man of medium build but his grim voice belied his mild appearance.

"Young man, what have you done to my receptionist?"

He came to stand beside the trembling girl and laid his hand on her shoulder protectively. Then he spied the picture. Picking it up he studied it briefly before lifting perplexed eyes to first Linn's face and then to Eric. "Where did this come from?"

Eric extracted a card from an inside coat pocket, and handed it to the doctor. "My name is Eric Ford. I work for the Randolph Realty and Development Company. Clay Randolph, the owner, is both my boss and good friend. Clay's wife disappeared three years ago when they had only been married six months. That picture, Doctor, was given to me by Clay and Linn shortly before her disappearance."

In a quiet voice the doctor asked, "Where did she live? Near here?"

"No, about a hundred and fifty miles up the river near Elktown. The Randolph estate is on the river. At the time Mrs. Randolph disappeared a canoe also came up missing. So it was presumed she had drowned. There is a long stretch of rough water, filled with treacherous rocks, just this side of Elktown. No one thought there was a possibility that Linn could have survived a trip in a canoe through that "whitewater." It takes skilled boaters to shoot those rapids. A long search was made but it turned up neither her body nor the canoe. Clay has thought his wife dead for almost three years."

He paused as if to study the expressions of the two before him. Then continued. . .

"I'm on vacation. Planned to fish at a lake near here. A short while ago I was driving through town and I saw your receptionist and followed her. This is Clay Randolph's wife, isn't it?"

"I don't know," the doctor replied. He laid a gentle hand

on the girl's arm. "Linn, let's talk with this young man." A long shudder shook the girl. "Linn," he spoke softly now, "you do want to know, don't you?"

Another tremor shook the girl. She spoke in a choked voice. "I—I don't know. I—I'm so afraid—so very afraid."

"Listen to me," the doctor spoke crisply, "Facts banish fear. Let's get to the bottom of this once and for all. We'll close the office and go across the street to the cafe and talk. Agreed?"

The girl drew a long quavering sigh. "Very well, I'll get my purse." She vanished into a small room nearby.

"What is she afraid of?" Eric asked in a puzzled tone.

"That's what we hope to find out," Doctor Glover said.

2

The telephone was ringing as Clay Randolph came from his room and clattered down the circular stairway. He was a tall man of almost lanky build, with a handsome thatch of dark, reddish-brown hair, styled carefully over his high, strong forehead; piercing hazel eyes and a firm, square jaw bespoke a stubborn will.

"Clay, it's for you," his mother called.

Clay paused with a hand on the doorknob and an irritated frown on his handsome face. "Tell whoever it is that I'll return the call later. I'm late." He vanished through the door without a backward glance.

He was backing his creme and red Mercedes Benz from the garage when his mother called from the side door. "It's Eric Ford. He said it was extremely important."

Leaving the car running, Clay dashed back into the house. "It had better be important!" He snatched up the offending instrument. "Hello, Eric. What's the problem?"

"Hi, Clay. Get a good hold on something. I've found your wife!"

The color slowly drained from his face and Clay spoke in a strangled voice. "You've what?"

Eric was apologetic. "I know this is a shock. I should have come on a little slower. I—"

"Are you trying to tell me that Linn is alive?" Clay asked hoarsely.

"She's alive and well. Been working for a doctor in Aliceville. There's only one thing. She can't remember a thing of the past. The doctor said she had a concussion from a blow on the head. She didn't even know who she is until today. When should I bring her home?"

Clay hung up the phone a few minutes later in a dazed condition. His mother spoke to him twice before he came back sufficiently to comprehend.

"Clay, what is wrong? Tell me—tell me."

In a faltering voice Clay answered, "It's Linn. They've found her—alive. But she—she doesn't remember who she is or—or anything. . ." His voice trailed off.

Ethel Randolph was a remarkable woman. She recovered from the shock almost instantly.

"Clay, compose yourself! Can't you see through this? Doesn't this sound like Linn? Highly emotional, imaginative, given to dramatics. Remember, Clay? Remember what she is like?" The voice had grown bitter.

Clay slowly straightened up, his jaw tightened, his eyes turned steely cold. "I remember, Mother. How could I forget! Yes, I remember," the tone was hard and caustic.

Mrs. Randolph spoke briskly now. "When are they coming? This evening? Good. We'll get it over with. Let me handle it. You won't even need to see her. I—"

Clay's voice cut in, "Mother, I am perfectly capable of managing my own affairs. So please stay out of this."

"But son, I only thought to save you more hurt." The voice was softly pleading. "I beg of you, let me—"

"Mother, I must ask you to stay out of this! Is that understood?" His eyes were dark slits of anger, his tone obstinate and icy.

"Very well," with an offended air Mrs. Randolph marched stiffly from the room.

3

Linn felt very tired and drained. The drive was a beautiful one, winding through tree-shrouded hills and occasional green meadows, following the clear mountain river all so typical of the Idaho countryside. But Linn didn't even notice, her thoughts were in such turmoil.

What was ahead for her? What was her husband like? Would she remember him or would he be a complete stranger? Surely she would remember her own husband! But would she? So far, for three years no crack had appeared in that horrible blank wall of the past, not one.

And the fear she had of remembering! Was it fear of the unknown, or was there *something* back there? Something her mind refused to remember? The very thought of "remembering" set her heart to pounding and her insides to quivering in stark terror. Why—why? She began to tremble.

"Linn," Dr. Glover was regarding her with concerned eyes. "Try to relax. There is nothing to be afraid of. Remember, child, we have prayed for this day. So meet it bravely. God will help you, you know."

Linn gave him a wan smile and said shakily. "I'll try. Truly I will."

"We are almost there," Eric said. "This is the beginning of Randolph property."

Pressing her lips with the knuckles of a shaking hand, Linn tried to concentrate on her surroundings. To the left of the road, the hills were wooded. On the right was the river. It was a beautiful river—clear and sparkling; green where trees lined its banks, clear as a mirror where there were open spaces.

Suddenly as the car rounded a gentle curve, Linn heard the voice of water crashing over rocks. These were not the first rapids they had passed, but from the noise, they apparently were the worst. The river was narrow and deep here. Gray, glistening rocks could be seen poking their wet heads through the tumbling, foaming, green waters.

"Rapids," Eric said. "You know I'm still puzzled how you got through all this 'white-water' in a canoe. It takes an expert to get through these waters in a boat or a raft." He glanced at the girl seated next to him. "You don't remember anything about the ride down river in that canoe?"

Linn shook her head. "I don't even remember the canoe. Dr. Glover said an old fellow found me drifting in the canoe. I was lying in the bottom with a big bump on my head. He brought me in to Dr. Glover in his old pick-up. Later when Dr. Glover came to find the canoe it was gone. Stolen, I suppose."

"Old Roscoe said it was a red and white canoe," spoke up Dr. Glover. "He found Linn in an eddy of the river, about 25 miles this side of Aliceville, and brought her into town."

The roar of water crashing over boulders and pouring through narrow channels continued for several minutes. Then the river was flowing wide and calm again, and the hills had gentled into softly rolling fields and woods. After a while Eric said, "There's the house—Grey Oaks."

Linn looked up quickly. Through a space in the trees she saw it. The house was large, white, two-storied, and roofed with gray shakes. There were several stone chimneys, here and there, and balconies on some of the upper rooms. Eric turned the car into a lane which turned away from the river and swept up a gentle slope. Winding through stately oak monarchs, they finally came into a circular driveway and parked before the mansion. There was a sweeping lawn, artistically arranged shrubs and flowers, and the magnificent old oak trees, for which the estate was named.

Dr. Glover descended from the car and helped Linn to

the sidewalk. "Does the house stir your memory in any way, child?"

Linn shook her head, numbly. Eric joined them and they walked together up the wide flagstone pavement toward the door.

Linn lifted her head and breathed deeply—not in pleasure but in desperation, trying to get some air into her chest, which felt squeezed and pressed out. It helped. She became aware of the crispness of the air, and the fragrance of the trees and flowers filled her nostrils, buoying her lagging spirits.

Wild thoughts began to whirl through her mind again. The people inside that frightening place she was about to enter knew all about her and all about themselves, and she knew nothing about either herself or them. Would they welcome her? What about her husband?

She had tried not to think of him at all. But the thoughts shouldered their way in now, unbidden and unwelcome. What would he look like? Would she recognize him—she was back to that again. Oh surely, she would recognize her own husband!

Her face felt hot and feverish. Her palms were wet, her fingers frigid. Her legs felt like jelly. Could she manage the last few steps to the door—and the ordeal that lay beyond?

"Dear God, please help me" she whispered softly as Eric rang the doorbell.

4

A middle-aged, plainly-dressed woman answered their ring. She admitted them unsmilingly and led them down the hall to a large double door on the right. She then politely ushered them into the large, tastefully furnished living room, seated them and asked them to wait. Linn glanced at the housekeeper's face as the woman turned to leave. There was recognition there; Linn was sure of it, and something else—dislike? Distrust? She wasn't sure. The expression had been fleeting but it left Linn uneasy and wary.

Linn saw Dr. Glover's kindly eyes resting upon her. He smiled reassuringly. She felt better. She and the doctor were seated on a large, high-backed couch, upholstered in rich red velvet. There was soft resilient carpet underfoot. Linn was vaguely aware of polished wood in the furniture and paneling, and of luxurious furnishings.

Eric went to stand before the large window overlooking the river. Linn rose and crossed the room to the window where he stood. The scenery was restful and verdant. The river, clear and greenish, flowed and rippled between white sand and rocks.

A voice caused Linn to turn. A young man, perhaps 27 or 28 years old, and an elegantly dressed lady entered. Eric spoke. "Hello, Clay. How are you, Mrs. Randolph?"

Linn stood petrified, not knowing how to greet her husband and mother-in-law. It was as she feared, they were complete strangers to her!

Mrs. Randolph advanced toward Linn and held out her hand graciously. Her voice was soft, cultured and sounded hospitable, but her eyes, gray and cold, were not.

"Linn, dear, this is a pleasant surprise. We feared you had drowned. We still can hardly believe you are alive."

She turned abruptly from Linn and extended a beautiful, manicured hand to Dr. Glover. "And this is the kind doctor who befriended Linn?"

Eric hastily made the introductions. Clay shook hands with the doctor. The gaze he flicked at Linn was inscrutable as he spoke an impersonal, "Hello, Linn." She managed a half-strangled greeting.

Linn's heart pounded almost out of control. What strange behavior for a husband who had lost a wife, searched for weeks to find her, and now seemed as casual about it as if a stray kitten had been brought home. What had been her relationship with this man before she vanished? If only she knew!

She soon found out!

After Clay and his mother had graciously seated everyone, Clay came right to the point.

Looking straight at Linn with stern, penetrating eyes he said, "Now Linn, let's hear your story."

Linn felt like a child, called up before the principal to give an accounting of herself. She sent a mute appeal to Dr. Glover with her eyes. He came promptly to her aid.

"Mr. Randolph, perhaps you will permit me to tell you how it was. This has been a very frightening experience for Linn. She does not remember a thing about the past before her accident. She only knew her name from a name bracelet she was wearing at the time."

The doctor paused for a moment, all eyes were upon him.

"Old Roscoe Cain, a man who does odd jobs about Aliceville, found Linn lying unconscious in a canoe that had drifted into an eddy about 25 miles this side of Aliceville. He brought her to my office, which at that time was in my home. Linn had a concussion from a bad bump on her head. She regained consciousness shortly but could remember nothing of her past."

Linn could sense that Clay was staring at her as the doctor continued. "My wife and I cared for her in our own home. By experimentation Linn discovered she could do secretarial work and we employed her as receptionist in my office where she has remained the past three years. That's the story, in brief."

Clay and his mother had sat still and watchful throughout the brief discourse.

Clay spoke brusquely. "Why didn't you try to find out who she was?"

"Because Linn asked me not to. She seemed terribly afraid of something or someone and begged us not to go to the police until she could regain her memory."

"What were you afraid of, Linn?" Clay asked. There was an amused, sardonic gleam in his eyes.

Linn forced an answer from her stiff lips. "I—I really don't know." It sounded lame to her own ears.

Dr. Glover cleared his throat, "Mr. Randolph, I am Linn's doctor as well as her employer. Linn will never be a whole, complete person until she remembers the past, good or bad. I don't know how things were between you and your wife but I feel that Linn should live here in her old environment while she tries to regain her memory."

It was Mrs. Randolph who answered, or rather cried out, "No! Oh no! That is quite impossible! Linn and Clay separated just before she disappeared, though Linn had not moved out." She was getting more and more agitated, working a tiny white handkerchief between tense fingers. "Since no sign of Linn could be found, we presumed her dead. Clay is—or was—to be married in a week to a lovely high-bred girl he has known most of his life." Her voice was rising. "I will not allow—"

Abruptly Clay's voice, cutting and commanding, broke in. "Mother! Please let me handle this!"

All eyes were upon Clay and his mother, and no one noticed Linn as the color slowly drained from her face and a small involuntary gasp was forced from her. She closed her eyes, and a shudder ran through her body. She was remembering! A tiny crack, had appeared in the blank memory wall. That woman, Clay's mother, was beyond that wall, her voice high and shrill: berating, accusing, con- demning. Then the crack snapped shut and Linn was again conscious of her surroundings but shaken to the core of her being.

Clay's jaw was a hard, inflexible line. He spoke to the doctor. "Your request seems reasonable enough to me. It is the least we can do under the circumstances. However, what Mother stated is true. Linn and I had severed all ties." He turned toward Linn, a scornful smile twisting his finely chiseled lips, "As I'm sure Linn remembers very well. For the record's sake, let me say, that I don't believe a word of this amnesia rot. I don't know what your game is, Linn, but we'll play it with you for a month. But after that—well, there will be a divorce to see to. I've got a future, all planned out, that I'd like to get back to. Fair enough, Linn? Doctor?"

Linn mumbled an incoherent answer but the Doctor looked displeased and said so. "Now look here, Mr. Randolph. Remember, Linn didn't come looking for you, your associate found her. It was my idea to come and clear up her past, if possible. If she is to be put in a deplorable, impossible position, perhaps we had better drop the whole idea!"

Clay opened his mouth to speak, but Linn, in control of herself again, stopped him. "Please, I would like to stay! I will try not to get in everyone's way, but I have a feeling I can remember the past here. Whether Mr. Randolph believes me or not is immaterial. I have committed myself to finding my past and I want to go through with it." She was absolutely calm now, to Dr. Glover's utter amazement.

Mrs. Randolph had sat quietly, but now she jumped up, murmering something about refreshments, and hurried from the room.

Dr. Glover looked at Linn with concern. "You are sure this is what you want?"

"Absolutely," affirmed Linn.

If Clay was upset that Linn had decided to stay, he hid it admirably. Now he was the perfect, affable host.

"Fine, since that's settled, let's see what happened to those refreshments." He touched a buzzer and almost immediately Mrs. Gray, the housekeeper, came with a cart laden with drinks and pastries. She paused near her employer to deliver a message.

"Mrs. Randolph asked you to excuse her to the guests. She has gone to her room. One of those sick headaches that comes on her suddenly."

As Mrs. Gray turned to leave after serving the guests, Clay stopped her.

"Mrs. Gray, Linn will be a guest here for the next month. Please prepare her old room for her."

Mrs. Gray took her time about replying—to show her disapproval, Linn felt sure. Finally she said, "Yes, sir," and left.

The pastries were delectable but Linn found it difficult to swallow. What had she let herself in for! Could she bear to live for a month in a household where she was totally unwelcome? And what of the hard blow on the head that she had received? Did someone here dislike her enough to harm her? Had she been put in the canoe to go to almost a certain death in the rapids? But, wait—she must push such thoughts from her mind or fear would drive her away from this house before she found some answers that she needed badly.

Linn forced herself to concentrate on the conversation flowing about her, of fishing, hunting, and real estate. (Eric had already told them that the Randolphs had made a considerable fortune in real estate and land development.)

At last Dr. Glover rose to leave. Polite good-byes were said, then Dr. Glover and Linn walked to the car. Eric lingered a moment to speak privately with Clay.

At the car, Dr. Glover fished out Linn's two suitcases from the car trunk and slammed down the lid.

"Linn," he sounded troubled, "I don't like this at all. Are you sure you want to go through with this?" Before she could answer he went on urgently, "I'm not sure it is even safe, Linn. To put it bluntly, I keep thinking of that nasty bump on your head. If we only knew it was an accident or—or—"

Linn tried to laugh lightly, more lightly than she felt. "Doctor Glover, civilized people like the affluent Mr. Randolph and Mrs Randolph don't go around knocking people on the head to get rid of them. That happens only in books. There are clean, legal ways to get rid of unwanted persons nowadays—divorce."

The doctor laughed, "Okay, I like your grit. Remember to call Mother and me often, collect. Promise, or the good doctor's wife will have my scalp."

Eric had joined them and heard most of their conversation. Now he spoke apologetically. "I feel rather badly about this, Linn. I seem to have tracked you down and thrown you to the lions. But if there is any way I can help, I'm available. I still live at Grey Oaks."

Linn thanked him warmly. But even as she did so, a disturbing thought surfaced. Eric was Clay's friend. Could she really trust him? The thought left her feeling desolate, without an ally in this strange household.

5

Eric left to take the doctor home. Dreading to reenter the house, Linn set her suitcases by the door and walked down a path that ran parallel to the house, through a small flower garden and out a gate in a low wall to the sandy private beach beyond. The sun was just setting. The scene was very peaceful and acted as a balm to her spirit. To her left was a small dock that ran out into the water. A small blue and silver motorboat was tied there.

Linn walked slowly to the edge of the water. This was probably where she left her past. She was frightened. She tried to regain the peaceful feeling of a few minutes ago but questions flooded in. How had she come to be in that canoe with a bump on her head? Was it from this small pier that she drifted—or had been pushed? Did someone in that house want to get rid of her, or had it been only an unseen accident, carelessness on her part, perhaps?

Linn sat down on a rock near the water's edge. She trailed her fingers through the warm sand. Pulling her legs up and circling them with her arms she slowly rocked back and forth. The fading sun felt warm on her back. Her questions were unanswerable at the present. Birds twittering nearby, the gentle slap of water on the sand, the occasional distant sound of a cowbell gradually brought to Linn's spirit a sense of God's presence. God always seemed more real when the world was peaceful, especially at eventide.

Linn began to pray within her heart: for courage, for her memory to return, for protection from the real or imaginary "thing" or "person" that caused her fear of "remembering." She thanked God in her heart for friends like Dr. and Mrs. Glover, who cared for her like a daughter. So lost was she until she heard a voice she didn't know anyone was about.

"Linn." It was Clay, standing not ten feet away, watching her with amused eyes. She scrambled to her feet, feeling like a child caught in the cookie jar. Why did he make her feel this way, on the defensive?

Brushing her skirt free of sand, she looked up, trying to gain composure, but feeling somewhat like a long-legged gawky child before this handsome self-assured man who was her husband. His dark reddish-brown hair gleamed in the sun, the dark hazel eyes watching her seemed to smolder as with a bitter fire. The expressive lips were curled in a disdainful smile.

"As I stated before, Linn, I do not believe you have amnesia." He put up a hand when she started to protest. The smile was gone now and his next words took on a cutting edge. "But it is no concern of mine, really, whether you have amnesia or not. Our ways parted for good three years ago. I consented to allow you to stay here mainly for the doctor's sake. He seems genuine and I value the regard of honest people." The caustic implication that she was neither genuine nor honest sparked an angry and puzzled retort.

"What have I done that you are so—bitter? This is hardly fair, since I have no idea what you are talking about!"

The mocking smile was back. "Don't you? If you really don't, then try hard and remember. The experience won't be pleasant, I assure you."

"Now," the mocking light was gone from his eyes and his manner was businesslike. "You will have your old room, which I moved out of before you left. I am very busy so I expect to see you very little. Mrs. Gray will see to your needs. You will have your meals with the family. And I expect dinner should be about ready." He turned to go; then turned back. "We have another guest in the house—Bonnie Leeds. Remember her?"

Linn realized that he was watching her face closely. Under his steely-eyed scrutiny she felt her face grow hot. He turned away, obviously satisfied.

"Just as I thought, you do remember."

Remember? Linn trudged up the path, following that insufferable man. Remember? As far as she knew, she had never heard the name. She was angry and disgusted with herself for blushing guiltily, and furious with him for being so pig-headed, so conceited and—and even for being so handsome.

Before following that haughty figure in to dinner, she leaned on the low wall to shake the sand from her shoes and let her anger die.

She was a little alarmed to find her suitcases gone, but when she was shown to a large room on the second floor by the disapproving Mrs. Gray, they were there, lying unopened on the bed.

As she crossed the room to open one, she felt a small object under her foot and bent over to investigate. It was a small, inexpensive dress pin that Mother Glover had given her. She had packed it in tissue paper in the bottom of her suitcase. Someone had searched her suitcases! But why? She had nothing to hide but it was not a cheering thought that her privacy had been invaded. And for what cause, she had no idea.

Linn looked around her assigned room and gradually her apprehension faded. The room was delightful, perfect—designed exactly as she, Linn Randolph (she grimaced at the name) would have decorated it.

The room had two white walls and two walls with tiny sprigs of spring flowers scattered sparingly on a white background. The luxurious shag rug was gold, as were the draw-drapes over the large sliding door that opened onto the balcony. A gold draped window looked out over wooded fields.

The immaculate, shining bathroom was also done in white and gold. Expensive pieces of walnut furniture—a four-poster bed, chest-of-drawers, vanity, nightstand, and even a matching desk and chair—were arranged about the spacious, airy room.

Linn longed to examine everything thoroughly but could not, she knew. Dinner was served at 6:30 and it was five minutes to that now. She washed her face, ran a comb through her hair, and deciding against changing clothes, since she had so few along, she slipped out of her room and down the gracefully curving stairway.

6

When Linn entered the dining room, everyone was already seated. Clay sat at one end of the table and Mrs. Randolph at the other. To Mrs. Randolph's left sat, or slouched, an odd little man. One glance and Linn knew (from her experience in a doctor's office) that he was an alcoholic. As she paused in the doorway, he turned slowly to face her then straightened up somewhat and she saw he was not really little but his slouching posture made him appear that way. He was of average height but very thin. His whole demeanor was hangdog. His eyes were dull and listless, but strangely, as she entered the room, his eyes changed and for a fleeting moment strong emotion was registered there. Fear? Anger? He dropped his eyes to his plate quickly so she wasn't sure.

Linn moved to take the only vacant seat, on Clay's left. At Clay's right sat a stunning brunette. The beautiful creature had a flawless complexion, lustrous black hair piled high on her delicately sculptured head, exquisitely molded features, and dark, dark brown eyes, lined with thick black lashes.

"Linn, darling," the girl said much too "sweetly," as she rose to hold out a slender jeweled hand. "I heard you had returned. So our little prodigal has returned at last!" The words made Linn feel like a large, overgrown kid, in patched jeans at the presidential ball.

The beauty took Linn's hand in a warm, soft clasp as if to welcome a much loved friend. Linn glanced toward Clay. His eyes, resting on Bonnie, wore an expression of deep admiration.

Jealousy suddenly burst inside Linn like an exploding volcano; boiling, blinding waves washed over her. She was remembering again! She closed her eyes to hide the rampant, violent passion that tore at her. The crack in her memory wall was widening—widening—Through the crack was this girl—only now she was laughing at Linn—taunting, gloating laughter—and Linn was shaking with feelings so intense that she wanted to claw and tear that beautiful face.

She was suddenly aware of someone shaking her and calling her name. She opened her eyes and saw it was Clay who was shaking her. She was trembling from head to toe. Mrs. Randolph and Bonnie wore expressions of genuine distress.

"Drink," Clay said, and Linn felt a glass against her lips. The water tasted brackish but she knew the taste was in her mouth and not the water. The quaking slowly subsided and the room came back into focus. Linn had been pushed into a chair.

"Are you all right now?" Clay's voice revealed concern.

"Yes—yes, I'm okay," Linn said shakily. "I don't know what came over me."

The meal was an ordeal and as soon as it was politely possible, Linn escaped to her room. She laid down on the bed and tried to recapture the two glimpses of the past that had appeared so briefly, but her uncooperative mind remained obstinately blank except for those earlier meteoric flashes.

But Linn now knew something with a certainty. Things had transpired in this house that had left a deep wound in her being and her mind was afraid to remember. And another certainty: Clay's mother and Bonnie Leeds had played prominent parts in that traumatic past.

In an effort to jog her uncooperative mind to remember, Linn pushed back to her earliest recollections three years ago.

She remembered regaining consciousness in Dr. and Mrs. Glover's home. Those days were a little hazy but she remembered the fears with which she had awakened. Vague, nameless, terrifying fears that raged and tore at her sanity. They were double frightening because she could not remember a cause for them, or even if there was a substantial basis for them.

Those early days at the Glovers ranged between two extremes: hours plagued by nebulous, tormenting, shapeless fears to hours of listlessness when she wanted only to be left alone to die. What patience and love Mother Glover had shown to Linn—a total stranger! Hour after hour she had sat by Linn's side, soothing her fears and, drop by drop, instilling the desire into Linn's heart to live again.

It was through Mrs. Glover that she had learned of God and the power of His Word. Mrs. Glover had not pushed her religion on Linn but had shared how Christ can change a life, making it a joy and a precious gift. Fear and despair had receded before the Word of God slowly, as flood waters before the wind and sun, but just as surely.

Linn learned the twenty-third Psalm from hearing Mother Glover quote it softly in those terrifying hours of intensified dread and fear. The ninety-first Psalm became special, as well as others, but the twenty-third Psalm remained her favorite, especially the part that said: "I will fear no evil for thou art with me." She repeated it over and over on sleepless, fear-ridden nights and it never failed to bring blessed relief after a time.

It was not until months later, when she was well again and regularly employed in the doctor's office, that she received Christ as her Savior. But she knew she had really met the Good Shepherd in those hours of need and desperation. Her public acceptance had only been a confession of the faith that was already there.

Though fears still lurked in the recesses of her mind, the horrible hours of maddening, pursuing terror were in the past. Linn, at the doctor's advice, had come to this house to discover her past, good or bad, as the solution to banishing those subconscious fears forever.

She began to pray as she laid upon the bed with her eyes closed. As always, she thanked God for her faithful friends, the Glovers, and she thanked Him for bringing her to them. Without them, and their love and faith, she was sure her sanity could never have survived the terrible onslaught it had withstood.

She asked the Lord for strength and wisdom to deal with the problems at hand, and asked that He would restore her memory and sustain her through whatever it might entail.

Quieted and fatigued, she fell into a deep, restful sleep.

7

How long Linn slept she didn't know, but she was awakened by a soft tapping on the door. Half asleep, she went to the door. The moon shone in at the large glassed doors that opened onto the balcony, spilling a soft, ethereal light into the room.

She opened the door and saw Mrs. Randolph—her hair

in curlers, and wearing a long housecoat, with soft house slippers on her feet. Even in this garb, she still managed to look somewhat elegant. Mrs. Randolph uttered a soft "Sh-h-h," slipped in and closed the door soundlessly.

"No—no, don't turn on the light," she whispered in a conspiratorial tone. "I *must* talk to you and I don't want anyone to know. There is quite enough light."

Clutching Linn's arm with an icy hand, she drew her to the bed, pushed her down and sat beside her. Linn felt so bewildered that she didn't say a word.

The usual hostile light was gone from Mrs. Randolph's eyes, her voice was gentle and beseeching. "You must not stay here! It isn't safe." Seeing Linn's incredulous expression, she made a vague motion with her hand. "Believe me! I'm concerned about you and your safety. Don't think that blow on the head three years ago was an accident! It wasn't!" She paused, as if to let her words sink in. "You must go away— and soon! I couldn't live with myself if something happened to you and I hadn't warned you."

She continued as Linn's eyes widened in disbelief.

"Now, Linn, if you repeat a word of this to anyone, I will deny it all. But I had to warn you. Now I must go." She rose to go but Linn suddenly recovered from her surprise and grabbed her arm.

"Mrs. Randolph, I do so much appreciate your concern, but I can't go until I learn about my past. Will you help me? Anything you can tell me will help."

Her mother-in-law became very still, her voice sounding remote, "What do you wish to know?"

"Oh, so many things! How Clay and I met, what caused our marital problems." Linn saw her stiffen but rushed on. "What did I do that Clay is so bitter about?"

Mrs. Randolph regarded her fixedly. For a long moment she did not speak, as Linn waited breathlessly.

"I refuse to discuss my son's affairs except to say it was your possessiveness and your jealousy that turned him from you. Now I must go." She padded swiftly from the room and the door closed noiselessly.

Possessiveness! Jealous rages! Yes, Linn could believe that, from the intensity of the emotion she had felt when Clay looked at Bonnie approvingly at dinner. But she knew the feeling had nothing to do with her feelings for Clay now. Although he awed her, even fascinated her, she certainly felt no love for the stubborn, conceited male!

Wide-awake now, Linn had a sudden desire to get outdoors. It was only ten o'clock and the sky was lighted by a brilliant moon. Slipping on a robe against the chill of the Idaho night air, she stepped outside her door and paused, considering. Should she go down the broad, carpeted main stairway or the smaller back one? Deciding on the latter, she walked softly past several doors and descended the narrow darkened stairs.

She hesitated at the foot to get her bearings, and realized the kitchen was on her left. A light was there, so she stepped to the doorway. Mrs. Gray was vigorously kneading yeast dough. Perhaps, Linn thought, I can get some information from her. Mrs. Gray had her back to Linn.

"Mrs. Gray," Linn began timidly.

The housekeeper turned abruptly and a spoon clattered to the floor. She spoke sharply, "You scared me, sneaking up like that!" She bent to retrieve the spoon, a frown on her plain features.

"I'm sorry I startled you and I didn't mean to sneak. I just wondered if you might give me a little information."

Mrs. Gray turned her back to Linn rudely and began once more to knead the dough, disapproval evident in her every movement.

"Mrs. Gray, I'm not trying to get you to divulge any family secrets. I just want to find out about myself: where I came from, who my family is. Anything you could tell me would be a help."

By the derisive sniff that answered her plea, Linn knew the housekeeper had been informed that Linn claimed to have amnesia, and that she, too, did not believe her. She felt frustration and anger begin to rise. "I came here to try to regain my memory and no one will tell me anything!"

Mrs. Gray wheeled to face her, floury hands held in front of her. Her voice was curt and hard. "Miss Linn, I'll tell you what you can do. Go back where you came from and stay gone! While you was here before, this place was in an uproar most all the time! There ain't no place for you here. That's my advice to you!" She swung back to her bread-making.

Stung to the core of her being, Linn turned and fled out the side door and around to the front. Locating the little walk that led across the smooth lawn, she sped down it, out the gate and down the rough flagstone steps toward the river. When she reached the river, she sank down onto the still warm sand, put her head on her knees, and prayed for calmness. She would need a cool head and a thick skin to be able to remain in this place until her purpose was accomplished. Unquestionably, the people in this house had conspired together to freeze her out. Well, they would soon learn that she didn't run easily! Her fighting blood was up now. But she must be careful to fight God's way. If she began to lash out and react in anger, God could not help her and her plan to find her past would be defeated before she got started.

Linn rose to her feet, went to the water's edge and washed her face in the cold water. She must get back to her room and get a good night's rest. She grinned wryly. The war was on, even if it was a "cold war," and she would need every ounce of strength and every resource at her disposal to win.

As she started back up the path, she looked up at the house. Most of the lights had been turned off and she suddenly realized how quiet and lonely it seemed. Remembering Mrs. Randolph's earlier warning, a tiny prickle of fear ran down her back and she quickened her steps. Glancing ahead, she saw an indistinguishable shape on the low wall in the shadows. Alarmed, her steps lagged as she peered ahead, trying to discover who or what it was. She proceeded slowly and warily.

Abruptly, the form moved and the throaty voice of Bonnie Leeds called, "Come sit with me, Linn. The moon over the river is quite gorgeous from here."

Linn approached uncertainly. What was this girl up to? What did she want from Linn? Most assuredly, she didn't just want to watch the moon over the river. Linn seated herself, and Bonnie said chummily, "I heard Mrs. Gray refuse your very simple and reasonable request. I see no reason why we should not help you all we can. Is it really true that you can't remember any of your past?" Her voice was sweet, her smile gentle and sympathetic.

In spite of the faint warning bell ringing dimly somewhere in the recesses of her mind, Linn felt herself warming to the friendliness of this lovely girl.

"Yes," Linn answered candidly. "I can remember nothing of my past, except for two brief flashes since I arrived here."

"Not even Clay?"

"Not even Clay."

"You don't remember how you and Clay used to fight, and how jealous you used to be of Clay and me?" She spoke lightly as if it were a shared joke.

"No, tell me about it."

Ignoring Linn's words, Bonnie abruptly reached over and laid her soft hand on Linn's left hand which rested on her knee. "You no longer wear your ring. What happened to it?" she said carelessly, but Linn sensed this was not a casual question.

"What ring? I don't remember a ring."

"The star sapphire, of course. Don't tell me you don't know what happened to it! Clay said you were wearing it when you disappeared." Her voice had lost its honeyed tone.

"I don't know what ring you are referring to," explained Linn. "When I regained consciousness I wore no jewelry except for this name bracelet." She held up her right arm and the bracelet tinkled softly in the crisp night air.

"Do you suppose that fellow who found you stole it, or the doctor, or someone in the hospital you were in?" Bonnie's voice betrayed a mounting agitation.

"No, both the doctor and old Roscoe are quite dependable, and I was never in a hospital. There is no hospital in Aliceville. Dr. and Mrs. Glover cared for me in their own home." Linn spoke decisively. "No, Bonnie, I am confident I did not have that ring when I disappeared. But why is that so important to you?"

Bonnie hesitated for a long moment. "The star sapphire belonged to Clay's grandmother. In Clay's father's will he stated that the ring was to be worn only by Clay's wife. I will soon be Clay's wife so I have a right to that ring!" Her voice was defiant, challenging.

"Describe the ring."

Bonnie was thoughtful, remembering. "It was platinum with one large blue star sapphire. Clay had a matching wedding band made for you, also platinum with a single row of small blue sapphires. I don't want the ring he had made for you but I do want that heirloom star sapphire and I mean to have it, if it is still in existence!"

Bonnie jumped from the wall lightly. "I must go in now." She took several steps and then turned back, as if on an impulse. Her voice was a soft, friendly purr again. "Linn, darling, sleeping dogs don't bite but if you disturb them they could fly upon you and rend you apart. Someone found and rescued you three years ago but you might not be so lucky next time. Why don't you clear out of here while you are still whole?"

Linn gasped, "Are—are you threatening me?"

Bonnie's eyes widened in innocent surprise. "Of course not! I'm only warning you, as a friend." She turned and walked swiftly away toward the house.

Linn stood near the wall and watched her go. Cheery lights glowed in several windows of the magnificent old mansion, but Linn shuddered. No one in that house wanted her here. And yet, she must stay until she had regained her memory. But was she wise to stay here? Was she in real danger? Mrs. Randolph and Bonnie intimated as much. Even Dr. Glover had been uneasy about her staying here. If only she knew what had transpired in this house before her accident—if indeed, it had been an accident. Had she done some terrible thing that had turned the whole household against her? If only she could remember! If only she could remember!

Suddenly Linn came to the realization that she was out in the night, completely alone. If someone were searching for a time and place to harm her—! Her feet took wings and this time she didn't take the dark, back stairs. The front door was still open and she used it!

Back in her room, she carefully locked the door, secured the doors which opened onto the balcony, and drew all the drapes. Her heart was beating wildly. She paced back and forth the length of the room. Then stopping abruptly in the middle of the room she spoke out loud. "Linn, stop this nonsense! God didn't give you the spirit of fear! Get a good hold on yourself. If God wants you to stay here He will protect you. If He does not want you to stay He will make His will known, if you will calm down enough to listen!"

It worked! She felt her heart begin to slow down; her frayed nerves began to relax. She picked up her Bible, and opened it where she had it marked. It was her custom to read some each night before retiring. She was reading through the Bible and tonight her reading began in Psalm 35. As she read, she was amazed that it fit her case at hand so well.

"Plead my cause, O Lord, with them that strive with me . . . stand up for my help, O Lord . . . And my soul shall be joyful in the Lord."

She read it over and it became her prayer. As she prayed those words aloud, she relaxed, her fears subsided and she found she was very tired. Tumbling into bed, she was asleep almost instantly.

8

Linn woke to birds singing in the trees outside. A rooster crowed somewhere nearby. Though it was quite early, a soft light filled her room. Linn laid in bed, feasting her eyes on the beauty and luxury of her room. This room filled her aesthetic soul with delight and she felt warm and safe within its walls. Or was it the Scripture she had read the night before, when she had prayed David's prayer and put her cause in God's hand? She didn't know, but she felt safe and glad to be alive and in this lovely, golden room.

She jumped out of bed, wrapped a duster about herself, pushed open the sliding door onto the balcony and stepped out. Resting her hands on the balcony rails, she marveled at the beauty about her.

The sun was just peeking through the trees. Everywhere around was color: smooth emerald lawn; darker green trees of varying hues; flowers and shrubs a riot of every color and shade imaginable; beyond the brown and tan moss covered stone wall greenish-silver water flowed and rippled between beaches of smooth sand. Pungent, tantalizing odors, and the splash and murmur of the river were borne to her senses by the dew-laden early morning breeze. Suddenly Linn wanted to be out there: to touch, and smell, and taste. She had planned to unpack but it could wait!

Hastily she changed into brown, corduroy slacks, gold blouse, and flat-heeled shoes. She brushed her hair quickly, slipped on a gold head band to keep her hair in place, grabbed a sweater and hurried down the back stairs.

She thought no one was astir but just as she turned to her right toward the outside door, a voice spoke her name. Linn whirled around in surprise and saw Clay standing in the kitchen door. How handsome—and cocksure of himself—he looked. He was in casual dress: dark brown trousers, and a lighter tan short-sleeved shirt.

"Care to join me for breakfast?" His tone was casual.

Linn was surprised at the invitation but tried to make her answer casual. "If you are sure I'm not intruding."

"Not a bit," he replied with a smile. Mrs. Gray doesn't get up at this dastardly hour so we're on our own. The coffee's perking, the bacon's in the pan. You can man the toaster, if you like." He set dishes on the small kitchen table, and turned back to the stove. "Do you still like your eggs over easy?"

Linn turned in astonishment from the kitchen sink where she was about to wash her hands, "Yes, how did you know? Oh!—I can't get used to the idea that you know all about me." When he made no comment, she began her assigned job of buttering the toast. As she worked, she pondered Clay's change of behavior toward her. Was he up to something? Probably. But she had to admit that she was enjoying his company.

Clay set the plates of bacon and eggs on the table and poured the coffee. When they were seated, he spoke with a ring of sincerity in his voice. "Just because we are permanently separated we don't have to behave in an uncivilized or hostile manner toward each other. I'm interested in knowing what you have been doing these past three years. Would you care to tell me about it?"

Linn laughed a bit apologetically. "I'm afraid there isn't much to tell. Dr. and Mrs. Glover were, and are, very kind to me. They nursed me back to health and gave me a job as a receptionist. I have lived with them ever since. As the only doctor in a small town, Dr. Glover is very busy so we don't have much social life. We go to church on Sundays and Wednesday nights and that's about it. It is a quiet life but very satisfying."

"Why did you come back here if you were satisfied?" Clay's gaze was probing but not unkind.

Linn looked directly at Clay and spoke earnestly. "I really didn't want to but Dr. Glover thought I should. You see, when

I first was brought to the doctor, and for several weeks afterward, I lived in a state of perpetual terror. Of what I have no idea. It was only through the constant care and love of the doctor and his wife, and coming to know their God, that I was able to survive with my sanity intact."

Clay's tone was quizzical, "What caused you to be so—so—" He groped for the right words. "So upset and fearful?"

"Dr. Glover said it could have been the result of the concussion but it was more likely that I was on the brink of a nervous breakdown and the accident pushed me on over. Now I seem to have a deep-seated, morbid fear of 'remembering.' I can't remember a thing that happened before my accident."

As Linn finished, she saw that Clay's eyes had grown steely-cold and when he spoke his voice matched them.

"Linn, I'm trying to be tolerant but I cannot buy that amnesia story. It's too dramatic and imaginative, and it so fits something you would fabricate." He stabbed a finger in her direction. "You recognized Bonnie last night and were hard-put to control yourself from throwing one of your famous temper tantrums. Isn't that so?" His eyes were blazing with suppressed anger.

Linn quailed before his accusing rage. "I—I will admit that I had a fleeting flash of memory last night. It was almost like a crack opening briefly and snapping shut again. The same thing happened yesterday evening when your mother spoke the first time—just a flash—and afterward my memory was as blank as ever."

The fury had faded from Clay's eyes but they were now bleak, dark slits. "I don't buy that, Linn. It just doesn't wash." His words were clipped and hard. "If you have come back to try to insinuate yourself back into my graces, you are barking up the wrong tree. I've had my fill of lying, and stealing, and temper fits."

Suddenly Linn was furious. She stood up, spilling her napkin to the floor. Her voice shook slightly but her icy tone matched his.

"Clay Randolph, you are the most conceited, pigheaded man I ever met!" Her eyes were green icicles. "I did not come back here to inveigle you into accepting me back. I don't even know you and I don't want to! For the benefit of your exalted ego, your mother and your girl friend kindled my memory briefly, but you are as unknown to me as a stranger on the street! Everyone in this house hints and accuses me of dark, mysterious, heinous acts, but no one has the gumption to tell me one concrete thing about my past. What kind of people are you, anyway?" Her face was pale except for two bright spots on her cheeks. She turned and with an angry toss of her pale blond hair, walked swiftly from the room and out the side door.

Clay caught her at the gate in the wall. The expression in his eyes was inscrutable but his voice was apologetic. "Linn, don't go away mad. Perhaps I am being unfair. It's just that this whole thing has me puzzled and confused. I want to believe you, honestly I do, but in view of the past I—I—"

"I don't ask you to believe me!" Linn flung at him. "All I ask is that you, any of you, be a little cooperative and help me regain my memory. That's all I came for, and that is the truth whether anyone believes me or not!"

Abruptly Linn stopped, took a deep breath and spoke quietly. "I shouldn't have lost my temper like that. It's inexcusable and I'm sorry."

Clay's face mirrored unbelief and astonishment. "An apology from you? I've lived to see the incredible! Oh, you used to apologize by little overtures, but never by word. Never! You were always proud and stubborn. You never said you were wrong or sorry, and you never cried." It was spoken as a fact and not as an accusation.

"I would have liked to meet that Linn of three years ago," Linn said dryly. "To date, I have discovered she was a liar, a thief," she ticked them off methodically on her fingers, "threw jealous temper tantrums; she was proud and stubborn, had a wild imagination, and kept everything around her in a constant turmoil. In short, no one says a good word for her."

Clay laughed suddenly—a friendly chuckle. "Come on back in the house. We'll finish our breakfast, find some fishing poles, and head for the river. When we get there I'll tell you anything you want to know about the Linn of three years ago. We might even rake the old girl up a redeeming virtue or two." He swung away up the walk and then turned back. "You do still like to fish, I presume?"

Linn looked blank, "I—I don't know—but it sounds like fun."

Clay surveyed her in silent speculation for a moment, then turned away, speaking over his shoulder, "The fishing's better early."

A few minutes later they were on a little path that led upriver, going north. Clay had selected a rod and reel for her from a goodly selection, telling her it had always been her favorite. After capturing a quantity of wriggly worms, which he placed in a can of moist dirt, he had led the way to a well-worn path.

The woods were quiet and peaceful, resting to the spirit, as they wound in and out among the trees, never far from the crystal-clear river.

Clay called back, "I'm watching for poison-oak but haven't seen any yet. You had better watch, too. Don't want you coming in contact with that, as allergic as you are to it."

"I don't know what it looks like," said Linn. "I can't remember ever seeing it or having a case of it, either."

"George killed out all of it on this path because you came here so often to fish. It seems he did a thorough job. Haven't seen any so far."

They were a good way from the house, now—perhaps a half-mile or so. Abruptly they came out into a small clearing. Linn saw they were at the mouth of a stream which emptied its water into the river. Rough grass grew almost to the water's edge.

Clay knelt and began to bait their hooks. "The fishing is usually good here. Our land borders both sides of the stream and we put up 'no trespassing' signs." He glanced at her with a twinkle in his eye. "This used to be the refuge for the 'Linn of three years ago' when she got things in too big a turmoil at home."

Linn wrinkled her nose at him. "Please don't tease when you tell me about her."

"OK, you asked for it." He motioned her to a tree near the stream and sat down with his back against one nearby. "Sit there. This is not the best way to catch fish but one can't talk much and catch fish anyway."

Seated on the grass, with their backs supported by tree trunks, fishing rods between their knees and corks bobbing in the water, it was really quite comfortable. Linn watched the bouncing corks with interest, liking the dreamy, hypnotic effect they produced.

"Now—where shall I begin?" Clay looked serious and a bit grim.

"At the beginning—when we first met, I mean," said Linn. She waited with trepidation and bated breath.

"You were working as a secretary in the head office of my dad's real estate-development business in Lewiston, Idaho. Dad sent me there to begin to take over operations, as his health had begun to fail. Before, I had been managing a branch office in Whitebird. To make the story short: we met, dated a few weeks, and were married. I brought you here to live because Dad was very ill by this time and I wanted to be near him."

"Are you an only son?"

Clay nodded, "Dad and I were very close. His death was a real blow to me." His voice was soft, almost inaudible. For a few moments he was quiet. Linn waited, not speaking. She knew he was reliving bittersweet memories.

After a while Clay cleared his throat, his voice became almost businesslike. "We were very happy here at first, even though you and mother never seemed to 'hit it off.' But there were no open disagreements until Bonnie began to drop in now and then."

He glanced at Linn. "I must explain about Bonnie. We grew up together. Our mothers were 'bosom' friends. They attended high school and college together and after marriage they were still close, visiting each other often. Bonnie and I were engaged to be married when I met you. As can be expected, Mother was very upset when I married you instead of Bonnie, but I can give her credit, she never treated you ill, even when we moved into the house with her."

I'll bet, thought Linn, remembering the bitter outburst from this "saintly" woman at her initial meeting with her the day before. She didn't like the turn of the conversation so turned the subject back to herself.

"Do you know my background?"

"A little. You were an orphan, raised partly in a foster home and partly in an orphanage in Spokane. No doubt, they have records, if you care to check." His tone was faintly derisive and Linn knew he was still doubtful of her amnesia story.

"I'll do that," stated Linn, a little too emphatically, on the defensive. "Now," she spoke lightly, "you said I was a thief, a liar, and threw jealous tantrums?" She left the sentence hanging in the air.

Clay was watching her closely. His eyes had gone stony. She grew restive under his scrutiny and finally looked away and spoke crossly.

"Whether you believe my story or not is not the issue. You have made those statements, now please give me some details." She waited apprehensively, half expecting him to jump and go stalking off.

But instead, he picked up the story in a forced, expressionless voice.

"It was natural for Bonnie to visit our home. From the first you were jealous of her but at first you made no issue about it." Bitterness began to creep into his words, "I tried to reassure you but my words meant nothing. You began to spy on us and if you saw us together, you threw childish temper tantrums. Then you began to steal things–small items—from our guests, from mother, even from our housekeeper!"

Linn gasped, this seemed utterly absurd, so foreign to her nature. "Are you sure of this? I can hardly believe . . . "

Clay turned on her savagely and spoke harshly. "Sure? The items were always found in your room, well hidden—in ingenious places, I might add. I cringe yet at the humiliation this caused us. We got so we didn't invite guests anymore!" He lapsed into a stormy silence.

Linn felt sick but she had to know more. "But—couldn't someone have put those things in my room? Tried to frame me?"

Clay threw down his rod and stood above her, demanding in an angry voice, "My mother? Our house-keeper—who has been with us since before I was born? No, Linn," pityingly now, "I thought of everything, believe me. I couldn't—and wouldn't—believe it at first. But you were the only person always present when an item was stolen. Most of the time mother was here, but a couple of times she was away when I gave a dinner party. Bonnie was a guest here some but not on most occasions. Even our housekeeper was absent a week once when objects were stolen."

"But why?" Linn's face was white and her breathing shallow, "Why did I steal?"

Clay still towered over her but his voice sounded tired and his shoulders drooped. "Mother finally called the orphanage and asked some discreet questions. It seems when you were there you had a record of stealing things when you were under stress of any kind."

Linn could have wept. Not for herself but for that girl of three years ago. How insecure, unloved, and bereft she must have felt to resort to stealing.

But Linn was still not satisfied. Stealing and lying were so repulsive to her now, could she possibly have done these things?

Clay, his anger spent, had gone back to his rod and sat

down.

"Clay." She unconciously used his first name. "Did that—that Linn of three years ago confess to stealing?"

"Confess?" The words were spat out. "Confess? Never! Linn Randolph denied all—with violent temper tantrums thrown in. She never stole! She never lied! She never spied on Bonnie and me! Even with the evidence laid out before her she always denied everything vehemently, accusing everyone else—me, mother, Bonnie, even our housekeeper— of framing her. She swore and screamed." He paused and then went on, "But she never shed tears. I thought all women cried, but not Linn! I expect she thought tears were a sign of weakness. She never cried! Never, no matter how angry or hurt or upset she was."

"She sounded—sick" Linn whispered the word.

Clay's tone softened, "I thought so. I loved her beyond good sense. I reasoned with her—pled with her—to see a psychiatrist. Mother pled with her. All to no avail!"

Neither noticed that they were both speaking as if this Linn was another person, removed from them.

Both were quiet now, thinking their own thoughts. Linn tried to sort out in her mind the information she had just gleaned, of a Linn who seemed so foreign to her present ideals of behavior. She knew God had done much in her life and she had experienced the "new birth" the Bible told about. But could she have changed so drastically? Clay seemed sincere so she knew the "old" Linn he portrayed was the way he saw her, at least.

There was one thing about the "old " Linn that was true of the "new" Linn. She never cried. She herself had felt this was strange as the women she knew cried easily and uninhibitedly. Even when she first regained consciousness after her accident and nameless terrors had nearly driven her out of her mind, she had never shed tears. Though her mind had been in an anguish of despair and tormenting fears, her eyes were dry. Dr. Glover had urged her to cry as a form of release but she could not. Could not!

Linn realized suddenly that Clay was studying her again in that speculative intent way he had that was so disconcerting. As if he were trying to look inside and see what really was there, trying to solve the enigma that was Linn Randolph. She said the first thing that popped into her mind.

"What happened just before your wife disappeared?"

Clay sighed, as if the story was becoming tedious. "We had a big row. I'm not sure I even remember what it was over. Our lives were almost a continuous battle by then. Anyway the offshoot was my declaration that I was through with her—once and for all. The end! Finis!"

He continued, slowly, "I vividly remember her standing down at the boat dock, eyes sparkling fire, face almost as pale as her hair. It was at dusk. When I said our marriage was over, she really blew up—swearing and screaming.

"I asked for the engagement ring back and she refused to give it to me. I grabbed her arm to take the ring from her and she tore into me like a wildcat. I was already so mad that I was afraid I might do her bodily harm so I broke loose and left her quickly."

They both remained silent for a time. Then he resumed with the story. "I went to the house and when she never returned to the house that night, we began a search the next morning. We felt in our hearts that she had committed suicide because the red boat was gone but the paddles were still on the dock."

Linn spoke softly. "Why was the ring so important to you?" Linn saw him glance at her ringless finger and she knew what he would say next.

"Where are the rings, Linn?"

Linn stretched out her long slim fingers. "When I was found I had no rings on, only this name bracelet."

Clay dismissed it with: "I gave you that. The engagement ring is a very old, exquisitely fashioned heirloom. I had the matching wedding ring made for you, but the other ring means much in our family. We'll buy it back, if you will sell it, and pay more than it's worth for it's a valuable ring."

"I know, it is a star sapphire." At Clay's quick look, Linn laughed. "Bonnie has already described it for me and asked for it. But believe me, I do not have it and never remember seeing it. I'm sorry," she said when he continued to stare at her.

Suddenly Linn had had all she wanted of the past. She felt drained.

She got up a little stiffly and said lightly, "Let's call it a morning. Didn't catch any fish anyway." She began to reel in her line. Clay began to reel in also.

The walk back was a silent one and at the house Linn gravely thanked him for his time and went immediately to her room.

9

Feeling utterly spent in spirit, Linn refused to let her mind dwell on the disturbing facts she had been told about the "Linn of three years ago." She kicked off her shoes and laid across the bed for a few minutes to rest. Later she rose and resolutely set about the business of putting the few belongings she had brought in the closet and a large empty dresser drawer. When everything was in place she saw that it was still early, only ten o'clock by her wristwatch.

She was about to go out onto the balcony when a sharp knock came at the door. She crossed the room and opened the door. Gaunt, stern Mrs. Gray stood there.

"I came to straighten your room," she said brusquely and moved into the room. "I see I'm not needed. You always were a neat one." She crossed to the closet. "All the things in closets and drawers belong to you. Clay would never consent to doing away with them, even though we all thought you dead these three years. I'll air them for you if you like. They'll smell of mothballs."

Linn warmed to this small kindness, hoping it meant the formidable woman was softening toward her. "That is very kind of you. I'll help you. I do hope some of it fits, as I didn't bring much."

Mrs. Gray nodded curtly and set to work removing clothes from the closet. As Linn moved to help, a disturbing thought surfaced. Had it been Mrs. Gray who had searched her suitcases, and if so was it on orders from someone else or on her own? She pushed the thought aside. The remainder of the morning was spent hanging clothes on the line and looking through drawers and shelves. Most of the clothes fit. A fact that was very pleasing to Linn. Some of the garments were obviously quite expensive and well-cut and her receptionist's pay did not allow for such luxuries.

At noon Linn was called to lunch on the terrace, which overlooked a flower garden which was obviously the joy of Mrs. Randolph. Mrs. Randolph came at the last moment from the flower garden dressed in old slacks, wearing a floppy straw hat, and peeling off garden gloves as she disappeared inside to wash.

Clay, Ethel Randolph, Bonnie (the perpetual guest, it seemed), Mrs. Randolph's alcoholic brother, Arthur, Eric, and Linn made up the group for lunch.

Clay, aside from a cool "hello" to Linn, ignored her throughout the meal. Arthur sat in an alcoholic stupor, eating what was passed to him and taking no part in the conversation. Bonnie, dressed in a simple white sheath that showed off her beauty to perfection, and Ethel Randolph carried on an animated exchange of ideas for a soon-to-be social activity in which they were playing a prominent part. Eric, though he greeted her and cast her a friendly glance now and then, spent most of the meal discussing a business matter with Clay. Linn was very much the outsider.

Everyone was polite to her but the easy talk that flowed about her was never directed to her. A shy girl by nature, she was glad when the meal was over and she could excuse herself. No one urged her to stay but Clay called to her retreating back, "If you still like the feel of dirt, George is out back in the vegetable garden. I'm sure he won't refuse some help."

Linn mumbled a "Thank you" and escaped quickly. Following a walk around the house, she came to a cobbled path that led to the garden. She would meet this George, who she had learned earlier, was the handyman and Mrs. Gray's husband. She needed an ally in this place and from Clay's intimation the "other Linn" had helped George with his gardening.

Passing through an opening in a tall, clipped hedge, she was immediately at the edge of a neat garden. A strikingly small, shriveled older man was leaning over a tomato vine, a hoe in one hand. At her cheerful "hello," he straightened up and looked her over calmly before returning the greeting. She saw at a glance that he had a crippled left arm, rigidly crooked with a twisted hand. A smile came slowly to his lined face. He came across the garden toward her. His movements were without haste but he had a deliberate, purposeful air about him that she liked instantly.

"Well, Miss Linn, so you fooled 'em all and came back from the dead." The twinkle in his eye was friendly and a balm to Linn's trampled feelings.

"I just never was dead, is all," she said, smiling. "Could I help you garden a little? I don't know which is weeds and which is food but I can learn."

"You sure can. As soon as I finish picking these pesky worms off these last two or three tomato vines, I'll show ye what ye can do. You better go get your hat, though, tain't exactly cool out here and I can tell you ain't been out in the sun much lately."

Linn ran to her room with a lighter heart. She had one friend here or at least he wasn't an enemy. She quickly returned with the worn straw hat and garden gloves she had seen earlier in her closet.

Reentering the garden plot, she walked quickly to where the shriveled gardener was bent over, picking off fat green worms and squashing them under a heavy heel.

Glancing up at her, he spoke in a preoccupied voice. "I just heered old Sarah's cackle over in the hen house. If I don't ketch her, she lays an egg and then eats it." He motioned with his crippled hand toward a neat white hen house within a small fenced chicken-run. "Would you mind to scoot over and collect what eggs they is and beat Sarah to 'em?' As Linn hesitated, knowing nothing about chickens or egg-gathering, he continued, "Gather them in that little straw basket hangin' next to the gate."

Linn went, but very apprehensively. She wasn't sure how you collected eggs. Suppose the hen was still on the nest? She most certainly didn't have the courage to reach under a hen and get one. What if the hen was possessive about her eggs? But not wanting the little man who seemed so kindly and amiable to think her a coward, she went.

She found the basket and entered the gate. Several chickens were scratching about but at her entrance ran toward her, making chicken noises. She almost absconded but realized in time that they didn't seem vicious; indeed they seemed very gentle and circled her expectantly. She glanced toward George but saw he was still bent over, absorbed in destroying those voracious green worms.

The hens moved away when they saw she had no treats for them. Drawing courage, she walked bravely on into the hen house. She saw to her dismay that there were two hens on nests. Moving cautiously toward the nests, she did not see the small bundle of white fury until it struck her leg. Fear put wings to her feet as she turned and fled, the enraged monarch of the flock right behind her.

With the basket, she warded off the repeated charges of the little pugnacious white leghorn rooster, who considered her an intruder in his domain. With enraged red eyes, puffed out feathers, and flopping wings, he pursued her every step. Miraculously she finally succeeded in getting through the gate. The belligerent little king struck at the gate viciously two or three times and then flapping his snowy-white wings, the cocky creature rent the air with a loud triumphant crow.

Safe now, Linn leaned against the gate to steady her trembling legs. Her heart was pounding and her mouth felt dry and parched. Breathing hard she glanced toward George. He was bent over in an awkward, unnatural position, clinging to his hoe. Suddenly with great clarity it burst upon her what he was doing. He was laughing! Bent almost double, his shoulders were shaking with suppressed mirth.

Rage boiled up in Linn like a seething volcano. She marched over to the little man who was still convulsed with almost helpless laughter and spoke frigidly.

"If that is your idea of a joke, I think you are—are cruel and—and as mean as your hateful old rooster! He could have hurt me—bad."

At the last sentence, George doubled up again, howling with laughter—aloud now. Deeply humiliated and still trembly from her recent fright, Linn turned away and marched toward the garden gate. These despicable people! And she thought George was her friend!

"Miss Linn, Miss Linn," called George hurrying after her. She stopped and waited until he came up, wiping his eyes with a large, printed blue handkerchief.

He sounded contrite. "I am sorry," he said, his twitching lips belying his statement, "that I skeered you so bad. But it was plumb funny the way you came tearing out a there like the devil was after ye." His eyes still twinkled with laughter. "As fer hurtin' ye, old Ben couldn't a hurt ye. I keep his spurs cut, 'cause he's so fightery. You will forgive me, won't ye, Miss Linn?"

His apology seemed so humble and genuine that Linn's anger melted away.

"I guess so. I'm not hurt but my ego has sure taken a bruising. I hope no one else saw me. Everyone has enough to say about me without giving them anymore fuel."

George was no longer mirthful. His face was sober, his eyes keen and grave. "Miss Linn, that was a dirty trick to pull on ye, but it proved them all wrong, just as I figured it would."

Linn was puzzled now. "I don't understand."

"Everybody thinks that story of yourn, about not remembering yore past, is jest a yarn you made up. But tain't so. I pulled that same trick on ye once afore and I'm shore no one would never fall for the same trick, pulled exactly the same way, the second time. I'm right sorry I skeered ye so bad but this was the only way I knowed to find out if ye was actin' a lie." His voice was genuinely sorry.

Suddenly Linn felt relieved and warm. She had a friend here, after all.

"I'm sorry I lost my temper and was so hateful with you." She laughed a little shakily. "I really must have been funny so I don't blame you for laughing."

George regarded her gravely for a long moment from alert blue eyes and then stated flatly, "You've changed. The old Miss Linn would never had said she was sorry. Never! You wouldn't speak to me for two weeks after I pulled that trick before and me apologizin' all the time. Tain't only that though." He lapsed into silence but continued to study her in a puzzled way. After a moment he spoke musedly.

"It's in the way ye walk and the way ye talk. You have a peaceful look about you, like you have come to grips with yourself, and the world and you don't hold a grudge no more. What happened to ye, Miss Linn?"

Linn spoke quietly and sincerely. "I don't remember the other Linn, but this Linn met a Man named Jesus about three years ago. I don't know what I had been running from but Jesus gave me the courage to stop running and to try to find some answers. That's why I have come back here. Only, so far, I haven't found anyone who really believes I don't remember my past."

"I believe you," the old man stated. "Now," he spoke briskly, "I better get back to me gardening. If ye've a mind to help, I've a hoe jest yore size."

10

Tired, after working in the garden for a couple of hours, Linn went to her room, bathed and changed into one of her newly acquired garments, a becoming lime peasant skirt, white cotton blouse, and barefoot sandals. Opening the door softly, she glanced down the hall. Seeing no one, she moved quietly but quickly through the hall and down the back stairs to the outdoors. No one was about as she strolled down the gentle slope to the river, near the boat-docks.

A rustic porch swing had been hung in a tall old oak. Linn sat in this, slowly swinging back and forth. It was very peaceful. The sun filtered through the branches, dappling the ground; the river gurgled and murmured past; a gentle breeze touched her skin with a cool, feathery hand.

Linn had grown so drowsy she was considering stretching out in the swing, when suddenly she felt that she was not alone. She turned quickly.

Stooped, obsequious Arthur stood not five feet away watching her with blurry eyes, a silly, sheepish, apologetic grin on his face. Pity, mingled with revulsion, surged through Linn.

He moved to stand in front of her, uncertain but obviously with something on his fuzzy mind. For some unexplicable reason, Linn felt a wary, suspicious feeling creep over her. She shook it off as ridiculous. When he continued to stand there, she spoke.

"Did you want to talk to me?"

He shuffled his feet and shifted his eyes to above her head. "You shouldn't stay here. You are in danger." He motioned toward the docks. "You had an accident down there once." He glanced around him and his voice dropped to a conspiritorial whisper. "I'm not sure it was an accident. Better leave while you still can."

His words sent shivers down her back but she forced a laugh. "Of course it was an accident. Who would want to harm me?"

The look he turned upon her was reproachful. "If someone knew I had warned you, I might be in danger, too." He turned and began to shuffle away, muttering, "That's the way it is. Try to help and she don't believe me."

As Linn watched him make his unsteady way toward the house, fear throbbed in her every vein and for a few moments, in her panic, she felt like running from this place!

This was the third warning in her brief tenure. But reason gradually stilled her pounding heart and she spoke softly.

"Heavenly Father, tell me what to do. Should I run or should I stay?" Gradually peace came and she knew she would stay.

That evening was quiet and uneventful. Clay, Bonnie, and Eric went out early to a party in town. Mrs. Randolph pleaded a headache and ate in her room. Mrs. Gray served Linn a solitary meal on the terrace. Very early a thoroughly weary Linn went to bed and fell asleep immediately.

When she awoke the next morning it was with a feeling of uneasiness. Everyone seemed to be staying out of her reach so she had little opportunity to talk to anyone. Bonnie did not arise until noon and then breakfasted in her room. Eric, still on vacation, rose late and was off to fish. Clay alone was up early but this morning he left on business in Whitebird, without breakfast.

Linn tidied her room in the morning and helped George in the garden. She read some in the afternoon, took a nap and relaxed in the swing under the big oak. As the day progressed, her apprehensions slowly faded under the influence of the warm sun, George's kindly friendliness, and the ripple of the cold, green river.

Consequently, when the family all gathered for dinner that evening, she was at her best, casting aside her natural shyness, she joined into the conversation with ease, not talking a great deal but making a worthwhile contribution.

Later, after coffee and dessert on the terrace, Linn excused herself and walked down to the river for a few minutes to unwind. The moon on the water cast a magical spell over everything. Linn felt glad to be alive, even though she had learned nothing about her past that day. After a few minutes of the peacefulness of the night noises Linn felt sleepy and went to her room.

When Linn opened the door to her room, she noticed a sweet, unfamiliar odor. Glancing about the room she spied a dark green, pebbly vase on a small table, filled with lovely wild flowers and greenery. Hurrying across the room she gazed in wonder at the carefully arranged beauties.

Linn touched first one exquisite flower and another, reveling in the delicate hues, shapes, and heady scents of the wild blossoms, set off to perfection with three varieties of greenery.

This is the end of a perfect day, she thought. Someone who knows how much I love wild flowers has gone to the bother to gather and arrange this bouquet for me.

Too tired and happy to ponder long on the identity of her anonymous giver, Linn fell quickly into a peaceful, restful sleep.

Linn slept late the next morning, which was Saturday. When she entered the dining room, everyone was gathered for breakfast, even Bonnie. Linn seated herself and declared brightly, "I don't know who gave me the wild flowers, but they are lovely and I love them." Everyone looked at her but no one spoke. She felt a little foolish.

The food was brought in—a delicious breakfast of sausage, gravy, hot biscuits and wild strawberry preserves. As Linn ate, savoring the good food, she noticed her hands itching. At first she rubbed them unconsciously, but that only intensified the itching. Before the meal was over there were several tiny blisters visible on her hands and they itched fiercely.

Clay noticed her obvious discomfort. "Linn, have you been in the woods and caught yourself a case of poison oak?"

"No," she said in a puzzled tone. "I haven't been away from the house since we went fishing. Is that what I have?" She extended her itching hands for inspection.

Clay took one look and confirmed it as poison oak rash.

"But where did I get it? Describe the plant to me."

"You should remember," began Clay and then hesitated, apparently deciding against inviting disagreeable discussion on her amnesia story. "I'll describe it. The leaves are green—red in the fall—three in a cluster on a low bush. They look like oak leaves, hence the name."

"But where could I have been near any? I know there's nothing like that in George's garden or down near the boat docks."

A thoughtful expression came into Clay's eyes. "Linn, you spoke of wild flowers a while ago. Is there poison oak among them?"

"I—I don't know, I never noticed. There is some greenery."

"We'll soon see." Clay rose and strode swiftly away up the stairs. Linn glanced around the table. All motion and voice was still. A watchful quiet filled the air, but as she glanced around everyone began busily to eat.

Clay returned quickly with the lovely arrangement and set it on the table.

"That, Linn, is poison oak," he stated, pointing to several slender stems with limp, oak-like leaves interspersed among the blossoms.

Linn felt a little sick. "But—but why would anyone give me a bouquet with poison oak in it?"

Clay said nothing but stared grimly around the circle at the table. For a long moment no one spoke, then Mrs. Randolph cried out in a resentful voice, "Clay—you don't really think any of us would do such an unkind thing?"

"Someone did." Clay's tone was flat.

Bonnie tilted her gorgeous head back and smiled up at Clay. "Do you know what I think? I hate to accuse anyone, but isn't there a possibility that our dear Linn gave herself a bouquet of posies?"

"But—but" Linn sputtered, "how ridiculous! And give myself a case of poison oak?"

"The pain might be worth it if it brought about a desired result." Bonnie's voice was light and mocking.

Mrs. Randolph rushed in with, "Of course, Clay, doesn't it fit? If she could gain your sympathy and make us look bad at the same time she might stand a chance with you again."

Linn was aghast. This is unreal, she thought wildly. Her eyes swept around the circle at the table. Clay looked grim and indecisive. Eric toyed with his coffee cup, silent and watchful, eyes averted. Bonnie had a slight smug smile on her face. Mrs. Randolph, sitting stiff and tense, had her eyes on Clay. Linn felt light-headed and nauseous. How could these people make such accusations? Surely Clay wouldn't believe such utter nonsense!

Clay sat down heavily. "One thing I do know, Linn. You'll have to see a doctor quickly or you could end up in the hospital like the first time you contracted it. It isn't far into town and you can take your little Volks. It's in the garage. Have George get it out for you." He stood up again, "As for me, I've got work to do." He turned to go.

"But—but" Linn's stammered words stopped him. "I can't drive—at least I don't think I can."

Clay seemed to turn this over in his mind before he snapped, "Of course you can, but if you still want to play games, someone here no doubt will have time to drive you in." When he reached the door he turned back and spoke, his words heavily laced with sarcasm, "If you can't 'remember' who our doctor is, his name is Dr. Leslie Meers."

Linn winced and felt her face flame. If she had been the

crying kind this would have been a good time to cry and scream in pure frustration and bewilderment. But since she wasn't, she fled to her room, washed her face in cold water, and prayed for help to control her rampant emotions.

When the violent itching drove her downstairs a few minutes later, Eric was waiting at the wheel of a light-blue Volkswagon. He motioned her in and they were quickly on the road.

"Thank you so much for driving me in," Linn said gratefully. "Coming back, if I get some relief from this itching, I would like to try my hand at driving, if you don't mind, and see if I really can drive."

Eric nodded. He remained thoughtful but as they neared town he turned and spoke earnestly.

"Linn, I'm asking you, in the name of common sense, to get away from this place, and quickly. I'm not sure what is going on but whatever it is, it does not breed any good for you. Poison oak is uncomfortable but far from fatal. But if that bump on the head was no accident, and I believe it wasn't, someone here wishes you greater harm than a case of poison oak."

"But why?" Linn cried. "What have I done that everyone there hates me?"

Eric shrugged, "Who knows? But if I were you I would go now—today!"

"I'll—I'll think about it." Panicky fear traced a cold finger down her spine.

11

But Linn did not leave. Dr. Meers prescribed a shot, pills and a soothing ointment. Within a short time, the itching subsided. Strangely, as the itching subsided, so did her fears.

Lying in bed that night, Linn's mind refused to be still. She had seemed very tired but as soon as her head touched the pillow, questions she had pushed away all day crowded in upon her, screaming for attention and answers.

Who in this house disliked her enough to send her poison oak, knowing how allergic she was to it? It was not an accident, of that she was sure. The people of this house knew her well, far better than she knew herself. Was this another warning? A shudder passed over her. She pulled a blanket about her shoulders.

Who in this house was her enemy? She thought of each one in turn. Ethel Randolph and Bonnie were certainly not her friends. They both had caused her anguish in the past, she knew, because of the brief glimpses into the past she had received.

Clay was a paradox. He seemed to have no love for her, indeed even hated her at times, but she felt that he meant to be fair. But someone had deliberately turned him against her—or had she, Linn, turned him against herself by lying and stealing and throwing temper tantrums, as everyone stated? What did she really know about Clay for that matter? Perhaps he had just tired of her and plotted to get rid of her. She recoiled from the thought but would not allow herself to dismiss it. She was here to find out the truth about her past and conquer that black horror that pursued, haunted and tormented her and yet refused to come out into the sunshine to be dealt with.

The very thought of that nameless, fearful terror set her heart to pounding, and brought her up in bed trembling. She forced herself to lie back down and to breathe slowly and deeply, praying for help. After a time she was calm again.

She was very tired but questions poured in again. Had someone deliberately tried to kill her? Or had she accidently fallen into the boat—or perhaps she had gone for a ride and struck her head someway? No. She had left the paddles behind, according to Eric, so she could not have meant to take a ride. That was out.

Could she have tried to commit suicide? Clay had said they had quarelled and he had asked her to leave. Perhaps she had no longer wanted to live. A tremor went through her. Thank God, whatever the cause of her bump on the head and her hapless journey down that rock-strewn river, God had not let her die. And now she had Him, whatever else was ahead for her.

She thought of the other three people under the roof of this beautiful mansion. What of George? She felt he was her only friend but she wasn't sure she could trust anyone here completely. George was nice to her but he was an odd little man. He seemed to attend strictly to his own business. If she needed help, she did not know if even George would come to her aid. Certainly the others would not, and neither would George's wife, the disapproving housekeeper. The thought was not very comforting.

There was Arthur. Poor, drunken derelict. No danger there.

Eric. Linn had forgotten him. He seemed to be concerned for her, but for some inexplicable reason—or feeling—she did not quite trust him. Did he have reasons of his own why he wanted her to leave?

Grey Oaks. Grey Oaks had a homey ring to it but she felt it was a deceiver. This house was a house of enemies—her enemies. Or maybe there was only one enemy here. One who wished her, not only gone, but dead. If only she knew who. If only she knew why. She began to feel panic again and braced herself against it. She drew a deep breath, squared her shoulders, and spoke out loud.

"Linn, you came here for a purpose. Don't be stampeded. If God be for you, who can be against you?" She felt better and soon fell asleep.

The next several days passed uneventfully. Linn had discovered that she could drive, and Clay had put the little Volks at her disposal. (She wondered wryly if he didn't hope to have her out from under foot this way.) Her rash under control, Linn explored the countryside nearby.

The gravel road which turned off the main highway and ran past Grey Oaks led up over a hill and through lovely woods and green meadows. Fat cattle grazed in the fields, and the woods and fields abounded in wildlife, birds, and a furry, inquisitive creature, which George said was called a "go-down" because he could burrow so quickly and disappear. ·

George also informed her that the five hundred acres around Grey Oaks belonged to the Randolphs. Clay had a small, but very fine, herd of registered Charolais cattle. The rancher who leased their lands also cared for Clay's herd.

Eric, who was still on vacation, spent his days fishing; his nights with Clay and Bonnie at parties and social activities. Bonnie spent most of her mornings in bed, her afternoons at the beauty shop, shopping, or visiting friends. Ethel Randolph worked religiously in her flower garden, when she wasn't directing Mrs. Gray and George in their duties. George was an "out-of-doors" handyman, scarcely ever appearing inside. He took care of the large garden, the orchard, the chickens, a cow, and did the maintenance and repair on the yards and buildings. Clay spent several hours a day in his office on the first floor. Everyone seemed to go out of his/her way to avoid Linn, except George.

Four days after the poison oak incident, Linn went in to supper. Everyone except Clay was seated when Linn slipped into her chair. Mrs. Randolph instructed Mrs. Gray to go ahead with the serving as Clay was tied up and would be a little late.

They had been eating for perhaps five minutes when Clay arrived. After he had been served, he turned to Eric and spoke in exasperation. "That secretary of mine has sure put me in a bind. Oh, it isn't anything she can help. Her Dad had emergency surgery yesterday so she has to be away. I some-times use a couple of local girls but they are both unavailable and I have to have a secretary to go with me to Spokane tomorrow. I'm about at my wits' end to know what to do."

Eric said he wished sincerely that he could help but that his typing was a disgrace. Bonnie turned a sweet sympathetic face toward Clay and wished she could help. All were talking, when Linn, almost before she knew herself what she was saying, spoke.

"I'm a secretary. Remember? I'd be glad to help."

There was a moment of stunned silence as if she had proposed some unheard of thing. Finally Clay spoke with an unconvinced ring to his voice. "Can you still take dictation?"

Linn laughed in spite of herself. "I would be a poor secretary if I couldn't. However, if there is a doubt, let me give you a demonstration."

When he hesitated, she spoke gravely. "You were very kind to let me come here. I know I have been an imposition. If you would let me do this, perhaps it would repay you in at least a small measure. Besides, I have a small axe to grind. I would like to visit that orphanage where I was raised if there is time." Linn glanced across the table. Mrs. Randolph had her lips clamped together in a tight line. Bonnie's eyes, fixed on Linn, were smoldering black pools of undisguised hate! Linn felt her stomach lurch in dismay—and fear. She looked away hastily.

Clay, plainly relieved, broke the uncomfortable silence. "Say, I do appreciate this, Linn. I will pay you well, and of course your room and meals will be furnished, too. We will fly there in my Super Cub. We leave at seven in the morning. We'll be gone two days. And we'll see that you get to visit that orphanage," he promised.

Bonnie spoke up a little breathlessly, "Would there be room for me, too, Clay? It would be such fun."

Clay looked contrite. "I'm sorry, Bonnie, believe me, I am. The Super Cub carries only two passengers. But, I'll be gone for only two days and Eric will see that you aren't bored. Okay, honey?"

Bonnie allowed herself to be placated, but she never glanced Linn's way the rest of the meal.

Linn knew she had raised the ire of the rest of the household, but aside from coldly ignoring her, no one except Eric said anything. As they were leaving the dining room, he said softly, for her ears only, "Linn, I wish you wouldn't do this." His tone was urgently foreboding, sending a prickle of fear down her spine. That was all he said.

She went to her room quickly to avoid any further admonitions because she had determined to go regardless of what anyone said.

After Linn packed her bag, bathed and shampooed her hair, it was still too early to retire. Restlessly she wandered out onto the small balcony, leaving the door open.

It was a lovely night. Except for the soft, sleepy twitterings of birds in the majestic old oaks nearby, and the gentle sighings of the leaves, it was absolutely quiet. The stars glistened in their black velvet canopy; the air had a soft, moist feel to it. She filled her lungs with the heady, earthy, fragrant air, her nostrils quivering with delight.

Linn leaned on the rail of the balcony thinking of tomorrow. In spite of herself, she felt excited and exhilarated at spending two days with Clay Randolph. She told herself sternly that Clay would trample her heart into the dirt and laugh while he did so, but the excitement still lingered, though slightly subdued.

Her thoughts swung to the impending visit to the orphanage that she had grown up in. A tight little ball of fear formed in her stomach. Would she find out that she had a parent, or parents, or relatives living somewhere? Would she find part of her past tomorrow? She felt a little sick and wondered if her subconscious mind was remembering something it refused to divulge to her. Would that terrifying "thing" her mind was hiding be revealed to her tomorrow?

Well, whatever, she planned to go through with that trip to Spokane tomorrow. She squared her shoulders resolutely, drew in a deep breath, and turned to reenter her room. As she stepped to the door she heard a faint noise beyond in the room and her lights went out. She froze, petrified with fear; her heart hammered painfully. She pressed a trembling hand hard over her heart to still its pounding, and strained to hear. But all was still—breathlessly still. Was there someone in her room—waiting and watching for her?

Suddenly a jarring realization came to her. If someone were really stalking her, she was easy prey here on this open balcony, spotlighted by the stars and moon. She moved swiftly. In one gliding movement she was inside. She spun to the right and darted along the wall where she crouched noiselessly. She listened for a movement. There was not a sound. She began to creep around the wall toward the door, stopping often, straining to hear. A sudden alarming thought brought her to an abrupt halt. What if the skulker lay in wait for her near the door, knowing she would eventually be driven there, seeking the light switch? Changing directions, she crawled noiselessly across the room. There was a small lamp over her bed. Sliding her hand over the pillows, she snapped on the light. Staring about with wild frightened eyes, she saw there was no one in the room!

Breathing heavily, she stooped and looked under the bed. Only after searching the closet and the bathroom could she persuade herself that there was no one in the room. She flipped on the light switch and it flooded the room with light. Had someone come in just to turn off her light? But why? To frighten her?

Her eyes swept the room. Nothing had been disturbed that she could see. She took a step and felt a stick-like object under her shoe. She bent to examine the object and drew back in dismay. It was a twig of poison oak! Her mouth went dry and her hands felt wet and hot. Someone had been here all right. To leave this object of warning! She knew it was a threat! For one brief moment of panic she felt like screaming and screaming. She checked herself with great effort.

She began to recite the twenty-third Psalm, slowly and aloud. Mother Glover had used this therapy on her three years before when the "terror" stalked and tortured Linn nearly out of her mind. It had worked then and did now. She repeated it over and over, and over. At last her nerves relaxed and she slept.

12

At six-thirty, there was a soft tap on her door and Clay's urgent, "Linn! Linn! It's time to get up." When he heard her sleepy reply, he told her he would have coffee ready but to please hurry.

When she joined him at the kitchen table fifteen minutes later, she looked the part of the competent secretary. She wore a rust-colored jumper with a long-sleeved tan blouse, set off with an apple-green scarf at the throat. Comfortable, trim, dark-green shoes and shoulder-strap purse of the same color finished her ensemble.

Clay's smile was approving, "Well, Linn, you certainly look like a secretary. Are you all ready to go to work? Fine. Let's gulp our coffee and hit the airway."

Mrs. Gray's delectable homemade doughnuts and hot coffee were made short work of; their luggage was stowed in the little Volks, and they were on their way to the airport.

Clay was a relaxed, expert pilot. In the better than an hour that it took to reach Spokane, he briefed her on what his plans were for the two days and what her duties would be. He explained that although he had an office in Spokane there were old customers of his father that would do business with no one but a Randolph. There were several real estate sales that must be finished these two days. She was to do the paper work connected with these and also get out some letters for him.

Interspersed among the explanations of her work, were brief comments on various places of interest they were flying over. Two places that were similar but quite a ways apart made Linn glad she was flying. There were two portions of highway, one near Whitebird and one out of Lewiston. Each was a portion of highway that spiraled upward in a series of hair-raising horseshoe turns. Just looking down at them made her dizzy. She had no way of knowing that one of these held a harrowing experience for her in the near future.

Once Clay swooped down low between the sides of a rugged canyon to show her a herd of elk browsing on the steep mountain slopes. He explained that this particular canyon was rather inaccessible and there was nearly always a herd of elk browsing within its protecting environs.

Clay and Linn took a car to the Randolph Real Estate office, picked up a company car and loaded their luggage, portable typewriter, and briefcases and immediately drove to the home of a client.

Linn loved the work of a secretary, so the day was a day of pure delight for her. Clay was a good boss: courteous, clear in his instructions. He made every word and move count, yet was a relaxed, witty, exhilarating person to be with. Linn found herself wishing several times that day that she were really Clay's secretary and that their relationship would not have to be severed as she knew it must be soon.

With only a hastily snatched lunch break, they worked steadily until six-thirty that evening. Some of her work had been done in an office at the Randolph Real Estate office. That was where they were that evening when Linn finished the last letter Clay had dictated, folded it, and tucked it into its envelope. Clay checked through the neatly stacked letters and legal forms on the large desk, looked pleased and suggested they call it a day. Everything was carefully put away in two briefcases and these were carried to the car.

"Let's go check into our rooms at the hotel, freshen up some and I'll take you out for dinner," Clay said. "I believe you have even earned a steak."

Linn glowed under the praise. Again she wished this trip did not have to end so soon.

The next morning Linn rose early to have a few moments of communion with God before her busy day began. As she hurried to dress she ticked off the day's schedule in her mind: breakfast with Clay downstairs in the hotel dining room at seven; a client to visit at eight; when they were through there, she had an appointment to visit the orphanage, which she had called and arranged for the day before. Her stomach gave a couple of flip-flops when she thought of that impending visit. A piece of her past should come to light this morning. What would it reveal? She was especially anxious to learn if she had any living relatives. And she was also desirous to get to know that girl who had lived at the orphanage—whose name was now Linn Randolph.

The girl who walked into the lobby of the Northwest Children's Home at 10:30 did not look like an orphan. In a chic forest-green suit and a frilly lime and white blouse, fair hair held back with a lime band, she looked what she was— an accomplished, poised secretary.

Mrs. Martin, the receptionist looked Linn over curiously before informing her that Miss Forrest, the orphanage superintendent, was expecting her.

Linn walked over to the building indicated. The orphanage was an extremely large complex of buildings and playgrounds. The many children racing about seemed happy, noisy and normal. Linn relaxed somewhat. Perhaps this hadn't been such a bad place, after all. She chuckled to herself when she realized what a grim feeling she had about places of this sort: that they were institutions of stern attendants and austere surroundings; places where trembling children were incarcerated, worked, and abused—a Jane Eyre type thing.

The woman who answered Linn's rather timid knock could have fit into the Jane Eyre orphanage category, however. She curtly seated Linn in front of a large desk before seating herself behind the desk.

A tall, angular, bony, no-nonsense spinster, she looked Linn over for a long moment with never a smile. Almost like she is trying to determine if I am a fit victim to admit to her domicile, Linn thought wryly.

And then she smiled—and she was no longer an ogre but was a warm kindly human being.

"Ten years have made a lot of changes in you, young

lady," she said. "And they are all for the better. Now, " Miss Forrest was all business again, "Mrs. Martin said you wished to ask me about your life here. What do you wish to know?"

Linn told her briefly that she had had a blow on the head and could remember nothing earlier than three years before. By piecing her life together, she hoped to trigger her remembering faculties. "I wish to know if I have any living relatives, and I would like you to make Linn real to me as you knew and remember her."

For a long moment Miss Forrest was thoughtful, watching Linn. Then she said briskly, "Let's start with the facts. I have your file right here. Let's see, you were twelve when you came here. At fifteen, you were placed with a family as a "mother's helper." You were with them—I can give you their name and address if you desire—until you finished high school. The State Welfare Department paid for your training at a business school, and it looks like money well spent," she finished with a smile.

"Now for the question of relatives. Your mother died of tuberculosis. That's how you came to us. Your father could still be alive but I doubt it. He was a confirmed alcoholic—bad—who not only did not support his family but reappeared periodically to talk your mother out of what she managed to earn as a waitress."

Linn burst out with a breathless question. "Do I have brothers or sisters?"

Miss Forrest shook her head emphatically. "No. Perhaps you could have adapted to life here better if you had had. You do have an aunt that I know of. She is your mother's sister. She was frail, like your mother, and with a tiny baby of her own she couldn't care for you. Your mother had no other living relatives that we know about and your father was an only child. We could never locate his parents so I do not know if they are living. Certainly not in this area. I can give you the address of your aunt—she lives in Washington, a couple of hundred miles from Spokane. But your father vanished shortly before your mother's death and we were never able to find him."

Linn exhaled a long sigh. "I have no one then, really. But I do want the address of my aunt. Now tell me about myself. I don't even know what my last name was."

"Merry Linn Bell. But you weren't a very merry little girl when you came to us. In fact, I doubt that you ever were. I remember you well—tall, very thin, very serious, very lonely. You missed your mother terribly and could never adjust to life in an orphanage. So many children about distressed and upset you. You were a loner, always trying to find a secluded spot—and that's pretty hard around here."

Miss Forrest was silent again, deep in thought. Then she looked directly at Linn. "You had always been an above-average student so when you withdrew more and more into yourself and began to fail in school, we knew something had to be done. So we—"

Linn interrupted in a forced whisper. "Did I ever," she faltered over the word, "steal during that trying time?" Her green eyes fixed on Miss Forrest burned with an intense light.

A little alarmed, Miss Forrest rose and went to fill a glass with water. "Do you care for a drink of water?"

Linn waved it away impatiently. "Did I ever steal, Miss Forrest? It is imperative that I know."

But Miss Forrest took her time. She drained a glass of water, replaced the glass with tortoise-slow motions. She walked back to her desk and sat down before she answered reflectively, "It is odd that you should ask that. A lady called us about three years ago, asking questions about you and that was one of the questions she asked. I thought it strange, is why I remembered."

"Was it my mother-in-law, Mrs. Randolph?"

"I'm not sure. She certainly didn't say she was your mother-in-law. She said she was considering you for a job and it was very necessary for her to know if you were trustworthy."

"What did you tell her?" Linn waited breathlessly.

"Just what I will tell you. That for a brief time after you

entered the orphanage you stole several things. I think it was in rebellion at the orphanage; the children whom you could never escape; acute frustration and despair, at the intolerable circumstances in which you found yourself. They were petty things but always things that were special to the owner. But it was only a phase and it passed in a few weeks."

Linn sat motionless, as Miss Forrest went on.

"But the next stage was harder yet to cope with. You withdrew into a shell. You would talk to no one unless you absolutely had to. This passed also after a time, but not completely. You continued to do well in school, however, until the third year you were with us. I suppose you retreated into your books. Then in that third year you seemed to lose interest in about everything. I believe it was because you had always felt that the Children's Home was only a temporary thing and suddenly it dawned upon you that you were here to stay."

Linn dropped her gaze downward, obviously struggling in her turmoil.

"Anyway it became evident to us that you could never adjust to orphanage living so we placed you with a family with two small children. It was the happy solution. You took over those children and house possessively, were a life-saver to the poorly organized mother, and you all lived happily ever after. Your grades came back up and you graduated with honors from both high school and business school. I wish all our children had stories as successful."

"Did I ever have a relapse and—and take things again?"

Miss Forrest looked quizzical but answered emphatically. "Never. You were absolutely trustworthy and we and your foster parents trusted you completely."

13

By four o'clock that afternoon Clay and Linn were finished with all the business and on their way to the airport. Linn was tired but she felt the trip had been a success in every way.

Clay flew down Hell's Canyon on the return trip. The spectacular canyon wound through rugged mountains, its serpentine Snake River appearing like a flowing silver ribbon from the air. Clay explained that this area was a primitive wilderness area, reached only by boat and trail. Herds of sheep were occasionally seen and once, as they swooped down low, Linn caught her breath in wonder when a graceful doe, followed by a diminutive spotted fawn, left the security of the woods to drink at the water's edge.

Clay explained that there were thirty lakes in the Hell's Canyon area but that many of them were only accessible by trail. Though they didn't see any, Clay said he had seen huge, white shaggy, black-horned mountain sheep here several times in the past.

Clay lapsed into silence the last thirty minutes of their trip and Linn was content that he was. Linn was amazed at the deep feeling of contentment she felt. As if this is the way it should be—she and Clay together, sharing and working together. The feeling persisted even when she told herself that this "togetherness feeling" was just in her imagination and it would be shattered utterly when they reached Grey Oaks again.

But of one thing she was certain, and it was a very disconcerting thought, she found Clay very attractive, and unless she checked herself quickly, Linn Randolph was well on the way to being in love with her husband. (And with a husband that was not really a husband but one that belonged to another.) This amazed her, too. She was one who always moved into friendships cautiously and slowly. And she had not even liked Clay several days before.

After coasting to a stop, instead of getting out immediately, Clay turned around in the seat and sat quietly looking at her for a few minutes. Finally he spoke. "You have changed. You have kept all the attributes that were what made Linn so attractive and eliminated the bad points. What has happened to you?" he asked bluntly.

Linn's heart skipped a beat. Then Clay did find her attractive! She spoke quietly, in spite of a heart that was beginning to beat a bit too loudly. "As I told you before, I didn't know the old Linn. You all know her better than I do. But shortly after the doctor found me, I accepted Christ into my life. If there is a change in me, I am sure He is what makes the difference." She spoke simply.

Clay continued to look at her steadily. For another moment he didn't speak and then he said softly. "I am beginning to believe you, Linn. But God help you if you're putting me on. I went through that once and that's once too often." He sighed. Then he reached over and picked up her left hand, holding it between his own lean brown hands. Linn felt the strength of the man in his hands. He spoke again softly, almost to himself.

"Such beautiful hands, and yet so capable. The only thing that is lacking is the blue sapphire. Were you serious when you said you do not know what happened to it?"

"I'm truly sorry, Clay, because I know what it must mean to you and your mother, but I do not know anything about it. In fact, I can't even remember it. Perhaps when I remember again, I will know what happened to it. Do you remember if I had it on when you last talked with me, before my disappearance?"

Clay released her hand, leaned back against the door and closed his eyes. His jaw tightened and he grimaced as if in pain. "You had it on! I remember it all vividly. It was about dusky dark when I went down to the docks. We had a bang-up fight. When I told you it was quits with us, I asked for the ring back. Just the heirloom sapphire, as the platinum wedding band had been made for you and I considered it yours. But the blue sapphire heirloom ring has been in the family for several generations and it is priceless to us. You were furious with me and you really let me have it. You swore you would never give it up and it would be over your dead body if anybody ever took it away. I was boiling mad. I grabbed your arm to take it and you fought me like a tiger. I have never struck a woman but I was in such a blind rage, I knew my reason was about to slip and I didn't know what I would do. So I pushed you away and made for the house."

"Did I fall when you pushed me? Is that how I got the bump on the head?" The air was charged with emotion, but Linn had to know.

Clay opened his eyes and chuckled. "If you were unconscious, you were the liveliest senseless person I ever heard. I swear, everyone in a mile radius knew what you thought of me. I should have taped it but I was too mad. I knew some of the words you called me but some I didn't know were in the English language." He was teasing now, but she got the message.

"But how, then, did I get that bump on the head? Did someone deliberately strike me on the head and throw me in the boat thinking I would never survive the rapids?"

Clay looked aghast and then scoffed. "Of course not! To be frank with you, we all felt you had committed suicide. You would have been capable, in your frame of mind."

Linn spoke softly, "Or someone cracked me on the head and threw me in the boat and meant it to appear a suicide."

Clay stared at her in unbelief. "Let's be sensible. Who in my house would attempt murder? My mother, who is so soft-hearted she hates to see a mouse killed? Bonnie? She couldn't have taken you under if she had desired to, which I'm sure she wouldn't. Why, girl, you nearly tore me up and I'm a strong man. Eric? No motive. Mrs. Gray?" His voice was mocking now. "No motive. George? He liked you. My uncle

Arthur was there at the time, of course, but again, no motive. That leaves only me and I just told you, I left you still alive and screaming."

Linn remained silent for a moment, pondering whether she should tell Clay about her visitor of two nights ago but decided against it. Although he had thawed toward her, he still trusted the people of his household more than he did her. Besides, she didn't want to destroy the rapport she had enjoyed with Clay the past two days.

She said only, "Right away I want to go down to the dock alone where I fell into the boat, at about dusk. I want to meditate on all of this and see if it will trigger my memory mechanism."

"Okay, you do that, but before we go home, let's eat. I'm starved." So Linn's rendezvous with memory was delayed for another day because it was after dark when they got home.

As they neared the house, turning into the long drive-way, Linn felt dread and tension—and fear—begin to build up inside her. A foreboding took hold of her, draining away all the happiness of the past two days. What lay ahead for her? Someone here was her enemy. If she and Clay continued to make progress toward a reunion, she felt confident that real danger threatened her. And yet, though she knew that no one in this house really wished her well, she did not know where the tangible danger lurked. It was a nebulous, therefore terrifying thing. Since she could not put her finger on which person or persons were the threat, she felt trapped, not knowing from what direction to look for trouble.

Pleading tiredness, which was suddenly a reality, she left Clay downstairs and sped to the safety of her room. She called Dr. Glover. She had planned to tell him all about how she felt and of all that had happened thus far. So far she had not done so, fearful of alarming him. But after she reached her room, the fear strangely diminished and she felt it was foolish to upset her friends. So she just gave him a reassuring message and after a brief prayer, went to bed.

14

Linn awoke in the morning refreshed and with an almost giddy feeling of happiness. Probing her mind for the reason, she realized with a shock that she was in love with Clay—or well on the reckless way. Chiding and arguing with herself did no good, because her inner self agreed with all her arguments and then blithely wondered how Clay would act toward her when she saw him again. Her whole heart longed to see him as the body craves food.

"Foolish, foolish girl," she kept muttering to herself as she dressed carefully, giving special attention to her hair, brushing until it shone and her scalp tingled.

But she could have saved herself the extra effort. When she came downstairs, Mrs. Randolph informed her right away that Clay had gone away on a two—or three—day business trip. Ethel also told her, in no uncertain terms, that it was extremely unwise for Linn to spend time alone with Clay as he was engaged to be married and he would not change his plans.

Escaping as quickly and as gracefully as possible, Linn started down the path to the river, with intentions of a walk, but was halted by a call from Bonnie. Glorious black hair flashing in the sun, beautifully dressed in a peasant blouse of pale green with a matching swirling skirt of apple red, strands of gay colored beads about her creamy neck and with a large floppy hat swinging from one hand, she looked like a bewitching gypsy, confident, yet carefree.

Linn watched her smiling approach with mingled dismay and apprehension. Dismayed, because she knew she could never compete with Bonnie's beauty or poise, and apprehensive because Bonnie was never friendly with her unless she wanted something.

"Come, go into town with me, Linn. Clay is away and I

detest driving alone. Besides," she grimaced, "I'm a coward. I have a dental appointment and I need someone to talk to, to get my mind off that wicked old drill that the dentist tortures me with."

Linn hesitated, caution sending little prickles down her spine.

"Oh, come on, be a dear," Bonnie wheedled prettily. "I need someone to drive me back if I'm in pain. Please?"

How could she refuse? So Linn went, but a little buzzer of alarm kept nagging in her brain like a pesky mosquito, until they were out on the highway. The top was down on the sleek, expensive convertible, and the cool wind whipping their hair as they sped along soothed and caressed away the apprehension.

It was a glorious drive: warm sun, spicy, balmy breezes; seated in the floating luxury of the powerful convertible. They didn't talk much. Bonnie seemed in high, exuberant spirits as she drove fast but skillfully. She was a winsome, disarming companion when she chose to be, and today she chose to be.

Linn did a little shopping while Bonnie was in the dentist's office. As she browsed in a sleepy general store and leisurely collected a few small items, she silently scoffed at her earlier fears. You're too suspicious, Linn, she scolded herself. With Clay away, Bonnie had been lonely and in desperation; even Linn would do for company.

Bonnie was still in high spirits when she came out of the dentist's office. A little too keyed-up, Linn remembered later, but she suspected nothing now.

"Let's celebrate!" Bonnie sparkled. "I only had to have a cleaning job so I'm treating us to a steak dinner."

The only flaw during the perfect broiled steak dinner was that Bonnie was having wine with her meal, politely refused by Linn. Linn knew little about alcoholic beverages, but it seemed to her that Bonnie was having her glass filled too often. So Linn felt a vague sense of relief when the meal was over and they were in the car again. Bonnie did not seem to be affected at all by the alcohol, unless her eyes were perhaps a little too bright. She refused Linn's offer to drive with a teasing, "Afraid of my driving?" but went on to say quickly, "We social people can handle liquor. We get lots of practice."

The first warning that something was wrong came as they reached the crest of Whitebird Mountain and began the descent. Bonnie flashed a look toward Linn that puzzled her and left her wary and uneasy, a flash of triumph coupled with a certain wildness. What could it mean? Perhaps she had imagined this. Certainly Bonnie did not act wild, but very calm and confident, as she completed the first hairpin turn, a little fast perhaps, but definitely under control.

Then Bonnie looked at Linn again and fear hit her in the pit of the stomach. There was a wild glint in the glittering black eyes as Bonnie yelled above the whistle of the wind in their ears, "Linn, dear, I'm taking you for a ride like you never had in all your born days!"

They were swinging around another hairpin turn now, the tires screeching and it seemed to Linn that the car could barely cling to the edge of the road. As they swung around at a dizzying pace, Linn could see far down, down, down into the canyon below. She pulled her eyes away and felt she was going to be ill. They were careening around another turn now and Bonnie began to laugh, not a pleasant laugh, but high, shrill and mocking. It chilled Linn to the bone.

"Stop, Bonnie," she heard herself pleading loudly, above the roar of the wind. "Please stop. You're drunk. Please, please, stop before you wreck us."

There was no answer except another wild triumphant laugh. Linn began to pray as she clung to her seat, "Oh, God, don't let us wreck." She didn't realize she had prayed aloud until she heard Bonnie's taunting voice.

"And I thought dear little Linn was prepared to die! Don't stop saying your prayers, Linn, dear, you may meet that appointment before we get down this mountain." Her mocking laughter was drowned out by the noise of the tortured tires and brakes and wind as they careened around another turn.

Bonnie's words shocked Linn to her senses. Fear drained away as she realized that her life was in God's hands because she, Linn Randolph, was a child of God. A calm came over her and a curious joy. Oh, wonder of wonders, she was safe, sheltered in the arms of God! And the marvel of it all was that she was no longer afraid although the car was still lurching and rocking around the punishing hairpin turns.

Bonnie was yelling again, "So you thought you would come back and take Clay away from me again!" Her tone was vindictive and menacing. "Clay has always belonged to me. I claimed him as mine when we played together as little children. He never belonged to you! Never! Do you understand that, Linn?" She glanced at Linn and her eyes were malevolent slits of obsidian.

Linn did not dare answer her for fear Bonnie would lose control of the car, so she remained silent.

"Scared within an inch of your life, aren't you? You do well to be frightened. If you stand in the way of my marrying Clay, I'll make you sorry you were ever born. Remember what happened before? Well, remember this one thing. Bonnie Leeds always gets what she sets out to get. And I plan to have Clay Randolph!"

Bonnie fell silent and Linn was glad, for the threatening sinister words were beginning to induce fear into her heart again. What did Bonnie mean—"Remember what happened before?" Oh, if only she could remember!

Suddenly she realized that they were down off the mountain and were speeding toward Grey Oaks. Neither girl spoke again until they were parked in the sweeping drive. Then Bonnie turned toward her and Linn could hardly believe the transformation. The wild fires were gone from her eyes, and her voice was soft and silky. "Linn, dear, it was so good of you to accompany me. Such an exhilarating ride." With a tinkly little laugh, she moved up the walk, perfectly poised and controlled. Linn could only gape in astonishment.

15

Linn slid out of the car and stood on trembly legs. She stood looking up at the stately, beautiful mansion. After her spine-tingling ride, the house seemed to have a brooding, oppressive aura about it. In her mind, it had become the House of the Enemy. She didn't know if Bonnie was the person that had once tried to take her life. She sensed now that Bonnie was quite capable if it entered her mind, but that she was an enemy, Linn had no further doubt. She should go away and never come back to this sinister place, and the strange people in it, where she never knew who was her enemy. Dreadful danger possibly lay in wait for her if she remained. The terrifying ride had left her very shaken and uncertain.

Unwilling to enter the house just yet, Linn took the path to the river, winding down until it came to the dock. The two small boats were tied there. As Linn stared down at them, dark thoughts traced their way through her mind. Perhaps she had stood right here when someone had crept up and struck her on the head and tossed her into the boat and set it adrift. She gazed out into the water. It would have taken only a few minutes for the current to catch the boat and send it quickly down toward those death-dealing stretches of rocks and swirling water. How had she ever survived? She shivered.

Stooping, she picked up a stick and tossed it into the current. She drew in her breath sharply; the stick was quickly caught and swept swiftly downstream. She shivered again, the memory of the rapids a short distance below vivid in her mind. Again she thought, how did I ever escape? And suddenly her heart gave back the answer. God! God, who has His eye on the little sparrow, had seen her and steadied the boat and kept it upright through the tossing, sucking, violence of the turbulent stream. That had to be the answer!

If He had not helped her, she would not be here now, seeking answers to her past and —and, yes, she would admit it to herself, she would not be here hoping, hoping with all her heart, to win back her husband's love and confidence.

She thought of Bonnie's angry threatening words back in the car, "If you stand in my way of marrying Clay, I'll make you sorry you were ever born!" What could Bonnie do to her? I must be careful never to give her another opportunity as I did today, she thought. Was Bonnie all bluff? Had the alcohol stirred her to act so irresponsibly? Linn turned it over in her mind. No, Bonnie was not drunk. She had kept the car in control—barely, but under control, nevertheless. Was the wildness in her eyes cleverly faked? Or was that the real Bonnie and her sweetness and gentleness faked? Linn could not decide.

Linn turned and walked away from the water. She was suddenly tired. She walked the few steps to a low stone wall that was built ten or twelve feet from the water's edge. Beside the path that led up to the house, there was a bench of the same natural stone built next to the wall. Linn sank down on the seat, feeling drained and weary. She kicked off her shoes and stretched out on the bench. As she did so, she felt a strange sensation. It was something she could not describe. It was as if she was in a very familiar place and that this wall or bench held knowledge that she needed.

She sat up and studied the wall and the bench. They were of rough, untooled stones set in concrete—very ordinary. She ran her hands over the wall and the peculiar sensation deepened. It was almost like the game she had seen children play called "hot and cold." When the children were near the hidden object, the hider would call out "hot," and when they moved away from the object, the hider would call out "cold."

Experimentally, she ran her hands over the bench and the sensation lessened. When she touched the wall above the bench the sensation heightened. The sensation was almost like a quickening of the pulses in her body. She knew her subconscious mind was reacting to something it remembered but would not divulge to her.

She stood back from the wall and scrutinized the face of the wall. Was there something hidden there? She leaned over and carefully examined each rock and the cement around each one. She could see nothing loose or out of the ordinary. But when she ran her hands over its surface she felt that tingling in her being. She stood there for some time lost in thought. Maybe there was nothing hidden here; maybe the bench was some way a key to something. She concentrated hard but her memory remained adamantly blank. So intent was she that when she heard a faint crunch of footsteps on gravel she whirled around as if she were being attacked by werewolves. Standing not six feet from her was Mrs. Randolph's alcoholic brother, Arthur. He was studying her. How long had he been there?

Arthur's usually listless eyes were narowed to slits of concentration. He didn't seem disturbed when she reacted violently to his approach.

His tone was suspicious. "What are you looking for?"

His manner angered Linn. "I'm not looking for anything," she said sharply but truthfully. "I'm just trying to remember, and this bench seemed to strike a chord. But I don't seem to be getting anywhere."

"Maybe I can help," Arthur said. He came forward eagerly, and began to run his hand over the rough rocks of the bench. A fear shot through Linn like an arrow shaft. Was her reluctant brain remembering again? She felt she must get Arthur away from here. She did not know what was here but she must not let Arthur find whatever it was, if there was anything.

With a great effort she turned away from the bench and took a few steps toward the docks. "Arthur," she said. He ignored her and continued to investigate the bench from every angle. She went back to stand near him. "Arthur, perhaps you can help me remember. Where was the boat tied that I—went away in?"

Arthur seemed to be having trouble with his foggy mind.

He focused his blurry eyes on Linn as she repeated the question. A look of wary defiance dawned in his eyes. "I don't know nothing about it," he muttered.

"I didn't mean that you really knew anything about my accident, but if you could remember where the boat was tied, perhaps I could stand where it was tied and try to reconstruct what happened. A strong emotion flamed in Arthur's eyes, briefly. Fear? It was gone so quickly, Linn could not ascertain.

"You aren't getting me involved in anything," he muttered. He turned and moved away with his odd shuffling walk.

She watched him go with mingled feelings. Did poor old foggy-brained Arthur know something? She realized with a sudden panicky feeling that here was someone else that she could not trust and must watch out for. She turned and walked with leaden steps back up the little footpath to the house.

At dinner that night no one seemed to feel like conversation except Bonnie. She kept up a running, gay chatter. She even teased Linn a little about the ride that afternoon, calling her a scaredy-cat and played the ride down until Linn almost began to wonder if she had imagined the danger. Then she remembered the wild, reckless light in Bonnie's eyes and knew she had not imagined. She glanced at Bonnie, so glamorous and fascinating, and a dreadful, lost feeling came over her. How could she ever hope to win back her husband with such competition? The girl was an actress. She could be anything she wanted to be and make one believe that that was her true self.

Throughout the meal, Ethel Randolph said very little. She looked tired and drawn. Several times Linn glanced her way and saw Mrs. Randolph studying her with an odd expression on her face. The older woman would glance away quickly when Linn looked her way. She ate very little and before the meal was over, Ethel excused herself to go to her room, pleading a headache.

Later, as Linn passed the door of Mrs. Randolph's room, she had a sudden inspiration. Tapping lightly on the door, she received a weak invitation to enter. Mrs. Randolph indeed looked ill. She was extremely pale and was lying on her bed with a damp cloth over her eyes. But when Linn spoke, she quickly swept aside the cloth and sat up with an agitated air. "I thought you were Mrs. Gray!" She waved a limp hand. "Please, I don't feel like talking now. I have a dreadful headache."

"Could I help?" Linn was amazed at herself for asking because she would certainly be refused. But she rushed on. "I worked for Dr. Glover and I learned from him how to relax tense muscles by massage. I would like to help you if I may."

Mrs. Randolph stared at Linn for a long moment, then grimaced with pain, and sank back against the pillow. "These headaches are unbearable," she said plaintively. "If you can help, I would be grateful."

At once Linn was the efficient small-town doctor's right-hand man. She had her patient lie on her stomach. While talking in a low, soothing voice, she gently massaged the muscles of Ethel's back and neck. She urged her softly to put away any worries, telling her that everything would work out. "Completely let your muscles sag, and sink down, down, down into the bed," she instructed. "Pretend you are floating, floating like a cloud in the sky. You have no weight. You are like a piece of down, floating floating, floating."

As she droned on she saw that Clay's mother was relaxing and obeying her instructions. She continued to massage, talking softly and soothingly. After a while she saw that her patient was sound asleep. She retired quietly to the door and would have gone to her room, but Mrs. Gray met her just outside the door. Her face was set in angry, disapproving lines. Linn put her finger to her lips and said, "She's asleep now."

Mrs. Gray looked incredulous, stuck her head in the door then slowly backed out. "What did you do to her?" It was an accusation. Linn felt a crazy impulse to laugh. Mrs. Gray could obviously not believe that she, Linn, could do anything of value. "Oh, just a little trick Dr. Glover taught me," she said lightly. Calling a soft "Goodnight" Linn went up to bed feeling that she had somehow won a victory.

16

Linn was awakened the next morning by a soft, insistent tapping on her door. Drawing on a robe, she went quickly to answer. It was Mrs. Randolph. She came in and sat on the edge of a chair near the door, looking uncertain and ill at ease.

"How are you feeling this morning?" Linn queried.

"I want to thank you for what you did last night. I suppose that's the first night I have slept without a sleeping pill in at least a week." Mrs. Randolph seemed genuinely grateful but Linn sensed this was not her reason for coming here, so she waited.

Ethel seemed to be searching for words. She looked at Linn steadily for a moment, started to speak then changed her mind. She got up and walked to the window. "I always liked the view from this window," she said irrelevantly.

Linn crossed to stand beside her. "The view is lovely and this room is lovely. I always feel so peaceful when I stand in this perfect gold room and look out at the beautiful things God has made."

Mrs. Randolph stiffened and moved away toward the door. Her face was away from Linn but Linn felt the next words she spoke would not be kindly toward her. The old barrier was back.

Ethel crossed the room and opened the door, turning with her hand still on the doorknob. "Linn, I appreciate what you did for me last night but if you had not come here I would not have been ill. You are making things intolerable here in this house. You must go away! I implore you to go back to your good doctor. Start a new life! You never belonged here. You still do not belong here."

Linn cried out, "Mrs. Randolph, I can't go until I find my past. That is why I came back. Please be patient with me just a little longer!"

"You came here to try to get Clay back, as we all very well know. I don't know why you stayed away so long but coming back now will avail you nothing." Mrs. Randolph's face was stiff with anger.

Linn fought to keep her voice low and controlled. "Please, Mrs. Randolph, I know you don't like me but I won't be here much longer—."

"No, you won't!" Mrs. Randolph lashed out. "I order you to leave this house. Today! This is my house also and I will not have you here."

"Mother, what is this all about!"

Both women were shocked to see Clay standing in the hall, just outside Linn's room. He was not due to come home from his business trip for a day or two. When neither spoke, he went on, "I decided to come back here to work up these contracts and letters, if you can assist me, Linn."

With no word of greeting, Clay's mother swept past Clay and marched down the stairs without a backward glance.

Clay watched her go and then turned back to Linn and said in a contrite voice, "Don't mind mother. I can't let you go now as I need a secretary again for a couple of days, if you feel up to it."

Linn hoped her eyes and voice didn't give away her eagerness. She tried to reply with real dignity. "I would be very glad for a chance to sharpen my secretarial skills, Clay."

The next two days were pure delight for Linn. She took dictation, typed contracts and letters. Mrs. Grey, stiff, with disapproval written in every line of her face and angle of her body, brought their lunch on a tray. At dinner, the carefully veiled animosity directed toward Linn was a living, ugly thing. Immediately afterward Linn escaped to her room.

If Clay felt or noticed anything, he gave no sign. He was a lively, efficient boss during the day and tried to draw her into things at dinner. But how, or with whom, he spent his evenings, Linn could not have said. She had put aside all but the present and was just enjoying being with one who was meaning more and more to her each passing day.

By the third day things began to change perceptively. For one thing, Linn inadvertently chose a dress from the store of her old things in the closet that she had not worn before. A thunderstorm had sprung up during the night and drenched their world. The new day was damp and chilly. She had noticed earlier the soft cherry-red dress with winged sleeves and square neck but it had been too warm to wear it. She found matching slippers and drew back her loose blond hair with a cherry-velvet ribbon.

She knew she looked festive and cheery, but she was unprepared for the look of shock in Clay's eyes when he looked up from his desk at her good-morning greeting. His face paled as he stared at her. He expelled his breath raggedly and seemed to be struggling for composure.

When he spoke after a long tension-filled moment, in which she had stood still, struck speechless with surprise at his actions, his voice was husky, unsteady, accusing and angry. "Why are you wearing that dress?"

Not understanding his meaning, Linn rushed immediately to her own defense. "But Mrs. Gray said the clothes were mine, that—that you said—" She floundered to a stop, knowing from his expression that she had not understood his meaning.

He went on as if he hadn't heard her. "You were wearing that dress when I saw you for the first time in Dad's office. You always wore it for special occasions because you knew how much I liked you in it." He shook his head as if to clear it.

Linn felt her face go hot with embarrassment. Clay must think she was making a grand play for him by wearing this dress. She stammered out in confusion and chagrin, "I—I didn't remember the dress. Please don't think that I—I—". She paused, not knowing how to mend her obvious blunder.

Clay continued to look at her with a quizzical expression. He seemed to be trying to fathom her motives. When the silence lengthened and she was about to protest again, he pushed back his chair and spoke in a curt voice. "Forget it. It's just a dress. We have work to do."

But it was not "just a dress," Linn discovered. She tried to bring their relationship back to the comradely rapport of the past few days but it was not the same. There was a strained, charged feeling in the air. Clay seemed distracted and edgy, and several times she saw his eyes upon her. She tried to work calmly but became so nervous that she was making mistake after mistake and that only added to the tension.

To make matters worse, Bonnie popped in three or four times with flimsy excuses for the interruptions. Obviously she was concerned with the fact her fiance was spending too much time in the secluded company of one, Linn Randolph. So it was with relief when Clay called a halt to the morning's work at about eleven. He suggested that they come back after one and clean up the last few bits of correspondence.

After discarding her bright dress and shoes and donning dark slacks and loafers, Linn went for a walk down to the river. As she passed the little stone bench she paused to run her finger lightly over the back and felt the answering quiver in her being. She lingered briefly but soon decided she was too "strung-out" to work on that mystery just now, so she made her way on down the river to Clay's fishing place.

But today she did not fish. She sat down at the water's edge, watching the light dancing on the crystal clear water. She tried to sort out fact from feeling and impressions.

One thing she was sure of. Linn Randolph was irreversibly in love with Clay. And she was sure that strong feelings were being awakened in Clay toward her. She found herself silently pleading with God to help her win her husband back. Perhaps she had been a fool to come back here but she knew she was not sorry. If only, if only, circumstances would not interfere and she could be Clay's wife again—not in name only, but truly "his" to share with and to love.

But the people of Grey Oaks were all against that, she knew. And it was more and more obvious that one of them had even tried to kill her. She went over in her mind what she knew about each one. Mrs. Randolph disliked her, but she could not imagine her trying to kill anyone. Mrs. Gray—Linn laughed silently at the thought she had about her. It would be beneath her dignity to commit murder. Bonnie would be guilty of desiring the death of one who stood in the way of any of her desires. But one couldn't imagine her dirtying her little well-manicured hands with an ugly weapon. She would get others to do her devilish work. Not George, that was certain. Bless his heart, he had been her friend when she lived here as the wife of Clay Randolph.

But still someone had attempted to rid the earth of Linn Randolph. Or so it seemed. Eric might be a tool for Bonnie to use. She had seen the feeling mirrored in his eyes when he looked at Bonnie. Quickly masked, of course, when he knew he was observed. But Eric seemed to like Linn, or at least he showed solicitude for her plight.

So who could have struck her on the head? Hmmm. She had forgotten one. Hazy, pathetic drunken Arthur. The thought was ludicrous. He wouldn't have the nerve! He did act suspicious, though. I would like to know if he knows something, she thought.

Engrossed in her own contemplations, she didn't hear the faint sound of footsteps on the spongy ground until a voice spoke her name. She spun around with a gasp and felt a little foolish to see Clay grinning at her as he pinned a squirming worm to a fish hook.

"Hope you don't mind my joining you. I brought your pole if you care to fish."

Still a bit shaken from her start, Linn shook her head. "I feel sorry for the worms and fish today."

Clay swung his line into the water and settled himself on

a rock. After a few minutes of complete silence, Clay spoke in a quiet voice. "Linn, you have put me in a bad spot. I don't know what I'm going to do with you. I have been extremely careful that I didn't get involved emotionally with you again. And I was doing very well—until today when I saw you in that red dress again. The feelings I thought were completely dead suddenly came to life with a bang." He turned to Linn with an odd expression on his face, almost apologetic.

"I had been engaged to Bonnie for two years when I met you the first time and threw her over for you. Here we are engaged, and you appear on the scene again. I can't do that to her again."

Linn sprang to her feet, her face pale. "I did not come back to try for a reconciliation. I came back only to learn of my past. I have no claims on you. I am making no demands. You are free to do as you please with your life." She turned swiftly to run down the path but Clay caught her and pulled her around to face him.

"You have no claims on me, Linn? My heart tells me differently. Darn it, I'm not making myself clear. I have obligations to Bonnie but I—I," his voice was warm and vibrant with emotion. She knew he would kiss her now and she waited.

Then just as suddenly as he had caught her, Clay dropped her arms and turned away. "It is I who have no claim on you until this mess is straightened out." His voice was unsteady. "Let's go see if lunch is ready."

Extremely shaken, Linn turned toward the path again and as she did so, she saw a flash of movement in the thick brush and trees on the slope above them. As she stared she saw another quick flash further away. Someone had been spying on them and was now running back to the house! A stab of apprehension shot through her being. The scene the person had no doubt just witnessed would add fuel to the strong feelings against her in Grey Oaks. She remembered Bonnie's barbed threat, "If you stand in the way of my marrying Clay, I'll make you sorry you were ever born!" Linn shivered although the sun was now shining brightly and the air was warm.

Linn did not tell Clay what she had seen. He would only have scoffed at her fears, she knew.

17

Linn did not return to her room until late in the afternoon because she and Clay went back to work immediately after lunch. She returned to her room at about four o'clock that afternoon. As soon as she entered her room she saw it! A little cluster of poison oak twigs, tied with the cherry velvet ribbon that Linn had removed before lunch and put away in a drawer!

Fear hit her in the stomach like a physical blow and she began to tremble from head to foot. She sank into a chair and covered her face with her hands. Her face felt hot and feverish. She didn't cry. Strangely, she never cried! She tried to fight down the fear but it only strengthened its hold upon her. This was another warning. She must flee this place. She was in danger. Every pulse of her being shrieked these things into her mind. Then she began to quote the ninety-first Psalm: "*He that dwelleth in the secret place of the most High shall abide under the shadow of the Almighty. I will say of the Lord, he is my refuge and my fortress: my God; in him will I trust. Surely he shall deliver thee from the snare of the fowler, and from the noisome pestilence. He shall cover thee with his feathers, and under his wings shalt thou trust: his truth shall be thy shield and buckler. Thou shalt not be afraid for the terror by night; . . .*" Slowly the words spread their healing balm through her being and the fear subsided.

Linn slipped down beside the chair and began to talk to God. When she arose from her knees a while later, she felt that she should not run away. Her sense of self-preservation argued that she was being foolish to remain but she seemed to have a distinct impression that to run away now would not be the answer. She had no way of knowing that within twenty-four hours she would question that this impression was from God.

Dinner that evening was a wretched affair. Clay seemed preoccupied and withdrawn from everyone. His mother was pale and listless; she left the table before dessert, complaining of a headache. Eric was taciturn and moody. Arthur was in his usual alcoholic fog. Only Bonnie chattered away, but this evening she sounded a little too festive, and therefore artificial. Linn was glad when the meal was over.

It was not quite dark and Linn was restless, so after dinner she slipped out a side door and walked down to the boat dock. Evening was a special time of day for her. Dusk cast a soft magic haze over the earth. The night was still except for the soft rustle of leaves, the subdued goodnight twittering of the birds, and the gentle slap of water on the sand.

Linn turned from where she stood on the shore and looked at the house above her. Grey Oaks did not look sinister tonight. Lights gleamed in the windows and Linn saw with an unbiased eye that it was truly a beautiful old mansion.

Linn turned and walked slowly down the shoreline. It was growing quite cool but she felt so peaceful and the world seemed so peaceful that she hated to go indoors. Suddenly she realized it was getting dark and she had wandered farther from the house than she had intended. She retraced her steps, walking rapidly to beat total darkness, because suddenly she did not want to be in the dark alone.

Almost running now, she thought she heard something behind her. She turned around but could see nothing. She had been a fool to go so far. She hastened on down the beach. There! She heard it again, unmistakable footsteps behind her. She stopped and turned around, listening. No sound. She thought she could see a dark figure down the beach but it did not move so she wasn't sure. She started on, and now distinctly she heard the footsteps behind her. She hurried on and the footsteps came on more rapidly. She stopped and called in a shaking voice. "Who's there?"

There was only silence. Fear beat in her throat. What should she do? Make a run for the house? And then a crazy thought. Whoever it was could have caught her already had he so desired. So this must be a scare tactic. She would turn the tables on whoever it was! Willing away her fright, she began to walk slowly on down the beach toward the path that led to the house. The footsteps came on, but slowly. A few steps from the path she suddenly turned and ran straight toward the dark pursuing shape. The trick worked. The figure hesitated and then turned and fled. She heard pounding footfalls and then the crash of brush as her erstwhile pursuer took to the woods.

Chuckling at this small victory, Linn slipped into the house and up to her room.

After her nightly prayer and scripture reading, Linn lay on her bed and thought things through. Since she had been in this house there had been many attempts to frighten her away but not once had she been really harmed in any way. This seemed to point to a startling fact. No one was trying to harm her or had ever tried to harm her. The bump on her head and the subsequent perilous ride through the rapids was only an accident or a scare tactic that had backfired. She laughed suddenly at the thought of her pursuer a few minutes before on the beach. Whoever it was had only tried to frighten her, and so it had been with all the threats, and warnings, and even the terrifying ride down the spiral mountain road. The thought gave her such relief that she was soon asleep.

18

Linn was surprised the next morning to see everyone down for breakfast at eight. Bonnie and Mrs. Randolph were going into town and Mrs. Gray planned to accompany them to grocery shop. Clay and Eric were off for the day to look at some property in another part of the county. No one invited Linn along but at least everyone seemed amiable this morning, even to Linn.

So Linn was left alone for the day, except for George in the garden and befuddled Arthur who made his shuffling way to his own little bungalow nearby to become inebriated, no doubt.

Linn thoroughly enjoyed her day. She straightened her room and did a bit of hand laundry. After helping George weed for a while, Linn packed a couple of sandwiches, a piece of cake, a book, an apple, and a pickle in a knapsack she found in the tool shed. Feeling very carefree and adventurous, she took to the woods. She took care to follow the little stream or at least keep it in sight so she wouldn't get lost. She had her lunch in a natural park of aspen and pine trees in a little clearing, seated on grass with the stream trickling over rocks nearby. The woods were alive with sounds—the gurgle and splash of the clear-as-crystal water, the song of birds, and hum and chirp of insects. After lunch, she rested her back against a tree and read until she became sleepy. Then, stretched out on the grass with her sweater for a pillow, she slept the sleep of those at peace with God and the world.

She was slightly alarmed when she awoke to see that the sun was very low and it had turned quite cool. However, it did not take her long to get back to the house, but it was dusk when she saw the lights of the old mansion. Perhaps it was the mood she was in but the lights seemed to welcome her tonight as she turned up the path to the house.

A door slammed and Clay came toward her. When he caught sight of her, he called, "Say, I was about to send a posse to look for you. George said you had gone out into the woods this morning and we were beginning to think you were lost."

At the genuine concern in his voice, Linn felt her heart beat a little extra hard. It was good to have someone care what happened to one, especially her good-looking husband.

Excusing herself to go upstairs to change and dress for dinner, Linn felt she was walking on clouds of purest heaven.

But when Linn took her place at the table, she sensed that something was wrong—not with Clay, but with Mrs. Randolph and Mrs. Gray. The formidable housekeeper was more stiff and reproachful than usual as she served the meal. Linn felt the woman's censorious eyes upon her throughout the meal until the food lost its flavor and her mind scurried about in confusion, trying to remember what she could possibly have done to further alienate the housekeeper.

Ethel looked pale and positively ill. She picked at her food and seemed to be waiting for something to happen. Linn grew increasingly jumpy as the meal progressed. She had a premonition that whatever was coming bode no good for her.

Dessert had barely been served when Mrs. Randolph laid aside her fork and announced, "Clay, Mrs. Gray has something to tell you."

Clay looked up in surprise at the ominous tone of her voice.

The housekeeper came forward from where she stood by the door where she had obviously been awaiting the summons. She stood near Clay, twisting her hands in her snowy apron.

"Yes?" asked Clay quizzically.

"It's like before, Mr. Randolph," Mrs. Gray stated. "The same necklace is missing."

"What are you talking about?" demanded Clay.

"My real pearl necklace is missing again, like it was several times before when *she* lived with us."

Linn realized with a shock that Mrs. Gray was indicating her, because all eyes were suddenly upon her. Just as suddenly that horrible bland memory wall was opening again and Linn realized that this was a repetition of something that had happened before. She felt a blackness of horror, fear, and a helplessness threaten to engulf her. She had stood up with a gasp when the accusation was made.

Now she grasped the edge of the table to steady herself as the overwhelming darkness, nausea, and fear washed over her again and again. She fought against it with all her being because she knew any weakness on her part would be counted for guilt. With great effort she managed to keep her eyes open, though the room was swaying and tilting. She forced her voice to speak and slowly the room righted itself and the blackness lifted, but then she began to tremble and could not control it. Linn didn't know what she had said but it must have been a denial because she heard Mrs. Randolph's voice shrill out.

"Of course she would deny it. She never admitted it before, even when it was proved."

Then Clay was standing by her, holding her hands that were shaking uncontrollably. His eyes were impenetrable but his voice was soft and warm.

"Linn, did you take the necklace? Tell me the truth."

Linn pulled her hands from his grasp. Amazement and incredulity turned her mind into a turmoil. Clay believed she had stolen that necklace! She heard herself stuttering a denial as she strove to cope with the shock and horror of the situation.

Ethel pushed back her chair. "There is one way to tell if she has the necklace." She looked full at Linn with icy eyes. "Will you permit us to search your room?"

"Of course, you can search all you like, but I did not take that necklace. Whatever would I want to do that for?"

"Because you are sick!" shot back a white-faced Mrs. Randolph.

Clay's mother turned and marched straight-backed up the stairs, followed by Mrs. Gray. Clay stood uncertainly, watching Linn. His face was ashen and his mouth a tight line of tension. He opened his mouth to speak, but when Linn, pale and with shaking voice again denied to the room in general that she had not taken the necklace, he snapped his lips shut and followed his mother up the stairs. Linn looked about the room. She saw Arthur's back as he beat a hasty retreat. Eric would not meet her gaze, and Linn knew he also felt she was guilty. Only Bonnie was calm. She did not meet Linn's eyes but she went on placidly eating her dessert as if the world had not crashed down upon Linn's unsuspecting head. Linn turned and fled upstairs. As she went, she knew with a dreadful certainly that the necklace would be found in her room.

When she stepped into her lovely gold and white room, she saw that a thorough search was being made. No one said a word as Clay and the two women pulled out drawers, looked under the mattress, and searched the shiny bathroom. Linn began to have hope, as place after place was searched and nothing was found. Mrs. Randolph and Clay seemed to have exhausted possible hiding places and were standing in the middle of the floor, sweeping the room with their eyes, when the resolute housekeeper let out a triumphant grunt of satisfaction.

The pearls had been neatly coiled in the bottom of Linn's bath-powder box. As Mrs. Gray lifted them aloft, strewing powder, Mrs. Randolph let out an exclamation. Clinging to the powder-covered necklace was a tie clip. When the necklace and clip had been dusted off on the housekeeper's apron, Clay spoke in a hard, flat voice. "It's Eric's ruby tie clip that I gave him for Christmas last year."

Linn had observed all this as one in a trance. She felt numb and drained. Now, her mother-in-law turned to her and spoke spitefully, "Do you still deny stealing these?"

Before Linn could speak, Clay put a hand on the elbow of his mother and Mrs. Gray and spoke firmly. "Please go now and let me handle this." He steered them out and softly closed the door.

As he turned back to her, Linn, in spite of her own anguish and confusion, felt her heart go out in sympathy to Clay. Strain showed in every line of his face and body. Anger lashed through her at the person or persons who were putting them both through this torture.

Clay went to her and took both of her cold hands in his strong warm ones. He searched her face for a moment before he spoke

"Linn," he began softly, hesitantly, as though he were feeling his way along. "I love you. I had thought that my love for you was dead, but yesterday when I saw you in "my dress" I knew I had only refused to accept it. I love you, Linn. I will stand by you until we lick this thing. We'll do it together. We'll get the best doctor available for you. And after we have conquered your problem, we will have a happier marriage than we ever had before. You will let me help you, won't you Linn?"

Emotions of all kinds surged through Linn's being as she listened to Clay's impassioned plea for her to accept psychiatric help: fear, anger, love, bewilderment, helplessness.

Suddenly she came to the realization that Clay was waiting for her reply. "Clay, you don't understand. I didn't steal that necklace or that tie clip. I can't help it if everything points that way. I just did not take those things!"

"But you saw where they were found. In your room, in your bath powder. Come now, Linn, be reasonable. At least acknowledge it when you're caught." His voice was kind and persuasive.

"Would you acknowledge something you didn't do? Of course you wouldn't, and neither can I."

Clay's voice took on a slightly impatient edge. "How do you account for those things being hidden in your room?"

Linn kept her voice calm above the panic and frustration she was feeling. "I don't know how to account for them. All I know is that I did not steal them or put them in this room."

"Are you accusing my family or friends of framing you?" A slightly mocking note had crept into his voice. "That's what you said the last time this happened."

Linn strove to be patient, to keep cool, to speak rationally. "Clay, I am not accusing anyone. I only know that I had nothing to do with placing those things in my room."

Clay's lips had thinned to a tight line, anger glinting in his eyes. "If you didn't put them there, who did? My mother? Eric? Mrs. Gray? Arthur?" His voice had turned cold and sarcastic. "You were always jealous of Bonnie. Perhaps you think she did it!"

In spite of herself, Linn felt her blood begin to boil under the cutting sarcasm, and lashed out. "Yes, it could have been your mother. She never liked me. Or Bonnie, who has always hung around the edges of our marriage like a vulture waiting for a victim. I didn't tell you about someone coming into my room twice and leaving warnings and about Bonnie threatening me if I took you away from her and trying to scare me out of my wits on the spiral mountain road. Just last night someone stalked me down on the shore. Your "household" has almost to a person tried to threaten, inveigle, or bedevil me into running away. And now this scheme."

Clay had listened to her outburst with hardly a flicker of the eyelashes.

"Well, that's quite a story. Why didn't you tell me before how you were being treated?" he said derisively.

"Because you would have acted just like you are now!"

"The same old Linn, when you get caught with the goods, you strike out at everyone around you!"

The words had an instant mitigating effect. Linn lowered her voice and spoke calmly. "Clay, I am sorry that I lost my temper, but the facts are still the same. I did not steal anything."

"Okay, let's skip it. Let's talk about Mother. You still have a couple of weeks left of the month I promised you here in this house. Mother is not well, and this past week she has been almost constantly upset because of your presence here. She has a bad heart and her doctor has warned that she must live a quiet life. Tonight Mother looked gray and sick. I cannot subject her to any more unpleasantness. You can understand my position, can't you? I don't like to go back on my promise to you or your doctor friend, but you can't expect me to jeopardize Mother's health . . . "

"In other words you want me to bow out gracefully?"

"That's about the gist of it."

Linn lifted her eyes to meet Clay's stern gaze and sighed. "Would you give me until Sunday, three days from now? I promise to do all I can not to upset your mother."

"Very well," Clay said crisply as he turned abruptly and left the room.

Linn thought about calling Doctor Glover about this latest effort to discredit her but decided against it. Three days would go quickly and they would only worry.

19

When Clay went to his room after seeing his mother settled comfortably for the night, he couldn't sleep. He walked the floor and mused. Could there be any truth in Linn's words? Three years ago he had had no doubt that she was a liar and a compulsive thief when she ranted and screamed and accused everyone. But this new, calm Linn was hard to doubt. Yet it filled him with dismay and repulsion to consider that any of his household would deliberately set out to frame Linn and to deceive him.

Bonnie was willful and used to getting what she wanted, but he couldn't imagine her stooping to low tricks to get her way.

And it was out of the question that his mother would lie or deceive him. She had never lied to him in his life. She hated a lie.

And there would be no reason for the others to try to drive Linn away. He thought of the threats that she had said were made to her. She said that nearly everyone had tried to get her to leave. That seemed preposterous. Surely the girl lied. But he was still too bothered to sleep.

He was staring moodily out the window into the darkness a few minutes later when there was a furtive knock at the door.

When Clay opened his door, George, looking apologetic, and uneasy was standing there. Clay beckoned him inside wondering what his visit could mean. George never seemed at ease in the main part of the big house and never ventured inside unless definite business brought him here. The Grays lived in a small apartment consisting of bedroom, sitting room, and bath at the back of the house and connected with the kitchen. They took their meals in the kitchen.

George came right to the point. "Mr. Randolph, I know it ain't a bit of my business but I got to have my say. Miss Linn is telling the truth about not remembering her past. I played a trick on her that I played when she was here the first time and she fell for it the same way."

He related how he had beguiled Linn into feeding the chickens and she had been set upon by the fierce little rooster. "She was scared to death just like the other time. She wouldn't a gone near that pen if she had remembered," he concluded.

"Maybe she's a good actress?" suggested Clay.

"Not a chance. She ain't the same girl that went away. I'd swear it on a stack of Bibles."

"Why are you telling me this, George?"

"Madge told me about her necklace being gone again and that it were found in Miss Linn's room, and that she had denied taking it. I never did much think Miss Linn did that stealing before, but I knew she didn't do it this time."

Clay leaned forward in amazement. "You know she didn't take it? Do you have proof?"

The old man looked defiant. "Only that she is different, and wouldn't lie or steal. I just know it, that's all."

Clay laughed shortly. "That isn't much proof. You always did like her."

The old man stood his ground. "It's all the proof I need. And I wanted you to know what I think. That's all I got to say."

He went out without a word. Neither of them heard the soft click of a door closing nearby, or saw the furtive figure that slipped again into the hall as soon as his footsteps died away and darted up the stairs and into a room there.

Linn tried to stay near her room the next two days but of course that wasn't possible all the time as she had to eat her meals in the dining room. But she meant for no one to have another chance to hide something in her room.

Clay treated her civilly but she caught him watching her in a disquieting way, but the rapport was gone. However, he did call her into his study the next morning and questioned her fully about the threats she had said she received. She told him everything she could remember, about the poison oak, the scare on the spiral mountain road, and the shore, and Bonnie's threat. She said that everyone except George had told her at one time or another that they thought it best she didn't stay. However, she conceded that perhaps some were just concerned for her or for the good of the rest of the household.

Nothing of significance the next day. Linn stayed in her room most of the time. But by the afternoon of the following day, before dinner time, she felt she must get outside for a little while or suffer a case of claustrophobia. She threw a sweater about her shoulders and tied a scarf about her head as a fine drizzle was falling.

She walked down to the water and walked along the

edge. She was glad of the warm sweater she had slipped on as the dampness seemed to seep into the very pores of any exposed skin, it was so fine and clinging. The sweater was one that Mother Glover had knitted for her, heavy, long and of a variegated yarn of red, orange and cream. Having the sweater on, with her hands in the deep pockets, gave Linn a curiously warm feeling. She was troubled, but how good it was to have friends like the Glovers, and their precious Lord that they had introduced her to.

As she walked along, Linn thanked God for her friends, the Glovers, and also for the friends she had in the little church they attended in Aliceville. Even if she never found out her past and Clay rejected her completely—her heart turned over in pain at the thought—she would still have Christ, the Glovers, and her other Christian friends.

She glanced at her watch and realized she had been gone longer than she had intended. It was almost dinner time. She turned her steps back toward Grey Oaks.

When she reached the house she ran in the side door and up the stairs. She quickly went down the hall toward her room but as she passed Bonnie's door, which was slightly ajar, Bonnie came out suddenly and they collided hard, in the hallway. As they almost went down to the floor, Bonnie grasped Linn's sweater for support. They righted themselves after a little scramble.

When she could catch her breath, Linn apologized, but Bonnie laughed it off with, "It's all my fault," and continued on down the hall. Bonnie was dressed in a becoming wine and white bathrobe, so she obviously was going to the bathroom down the hall.

When Linn reached her room, she went to stand at the window to watch the fine rain falling outdoors. It felt cozy to be inside, in her gold and white room. It even had a private bath. Clay must have loved her dearly in the past to have provided her with a luxury that no other room in the house had. She glanced about the room and, with a pang, realized that tomorrow, unless God intervened, she would have to leave this room—and Clay, perhaps forever. She pulled herself up short. She must stop being so depressed and get ready for dinner. Just at that moment she heard quick steps in the hall and a knock on the door. Crossing to open the door, Linn was surprised to see Clay at the door and, just behind him, his mother and Bonnie. Clay looked angry, Mrs. Randolph looked ill, and Bonnie's face was inscrutable.

Clay said sternly, "Bonnie said she saw you come out of her room just now and that her engagement ring is missing."

Linn was struck absolutely speechless. Before she could find her voice, Bonnie burst out accusingly: "I had taken off my ring to take a bath. I left it on the stand by the bed. As I was coming out of the bathroom, I saw Linn coming out of my room. When I got to my room the ring was gone!"

Linn stared at the three persons facing her in stunned amazement. She finally found her voice. "Why, this is ridiculous! I have just come from outdoors. Besides, I wouldn't go in Bonnie's room unless she invited me. I—I—" Her arguments sounded childish and foolish even to her own ears.

Bonnie turned dark, imploring eyes on Clay. "She probably hasn't had time to hide it in the room. Maybe it is still on her person." She turned to Linn. "Are you afraid to be searched?"

"Why, of course not! I didn't take that ring and you know it!"

"Very well," Bonnie said triumphantly. "Is it okay if Mother Randolph searches her, Clay?"

Clay's voice was set in stony lines. He merely nodded.

Mrs. Randolph moved forward obediently. Linn was shocked to see how haggard she looked. She thought in amazement, She looks like she could collapse at any minute; she is very ill; don't the others realize? Their eyes were on Linn and she knew they did not see.

Clay's mother fumbled clumsily in the pockets of Linn's sweater. Linn was so concerned for Mrs. Randolph that for a second she had forgotten about the ring—until Bonnie gave a triumphant cry and sprang forward, taking an object from Mrs. Randolph's fingers that she had obviously just taken from Linn's pocket. Linn could only stare, dumbfounded. It was Bonnie's ring!

"Well, Linn?" Clay's voice was cutting and cold.

"I—I don't know how it got in my pocket," she stammered. "It's the truth, Clay! I swear I didn't steal it. You must believe me!"

Clay's eyes were boring into her very soul, gimlets of contempt and hot anger. "Believe you, Linn. You ask me to believe?" He turned from her as if the sight of her repulsed him.

In desperation, Linn reached out to him, to plead with him, when she heard a low moan. Linn spun around to see Mrs. Randolph sagging against the bed, clutching her heart. Clay and Bonnie had also heard her groan. Clay was instantly at her side, easing her onto Linn's bed. He snapped at Bonnie, "Call her doctor. The number is on the front of the phone book."

He ran to the door and shouted down the hall for Mrs. Gray. She appeared at the head of the stairs almost instantly. "Get Mother's medicine," he ordered. The housekeeper disappeared, to return with it on the run.

"Slip this under your tongue," she urged his mother gently. Ethel complied although she was obviously in great pain.

Linn stood helplessly and fearfully by throughout the traumatic scene. As she watched the woman moaning and clutching her chest with convulsive fingers, waves of darkness and fear began to claw at Linn's being. She was remembering again. She started to resist it and then a new thought came to her forcefully. Before, she had always fought it off, not the remembering, but the accompanying trepidation, blackness and fear that came with it. This time she would cooperate and see what she could remember. She was shaking with the force that tore at her. She ran from the room and no one noticed her going as everyone was working with Mrs. Randolph. Bonnie had just returned to say that both the doctor and an ambulance were on the way.

Linn ran on swift but stumbling feet. She reached the yard and took the path down to the river. She was shaking so badly as she reached the bottom step that she clung to the wall just above the little stone bench, for support.

She was remembering. Dense, like fog, but remembrance just the same. Mrs. Randolph had been sick then too, not quite the same, but very sick. Perhaps it was just her nerves then. She strove to remember but it wasn't clear. But she had been very white and shaken and they had called the doctor. It had all begun over Linn stealing something. She struggled to remember what. She couldn't remember, but whatever it was had belonged to Bonnie, and Mrs. Randolph had searched her, and—strangely—it had been on her person before just as the ring was in her sweater pocket just now. For a crazy moment she wondered if she *had* taken those things. If not, how did they get on her person? Was she crazy and didn't know it? She knew that people with mental problems didn't think themselves unbalanced. She pushed the ridiculous thought aside, and tried to remember some more.

The shaking had subsided somewhat and she found she could still remember some things, vague, and shadowy . . . She was still clinging to the stone wall for support and now, as she shifted her grasp, she felt a stone move. An electric shock went through her. She lifted stunned eyes to the rock under her hand. That is where they are! They are not hidden on the seat of the bench or the back but under the cornerstone at the top!

Linn's hand trembled so that she could hardly remove the stone! She tore a fingernail in the process but didn't even notice. Her heart was beating like a trip-hammer. She knew what she would find here, unless—perish the thought—someone else had found them.

At last she had the stone worked out. She pushed her hand into the narrow opening and extracted a small, soiled handkerchief with the initials *L.R.* in the corner. With shaking fingers she peeled back the cover to reveal the contents. Two shiny circlets of platinum lay in her palm! One was a solitaire engagement ring with a large brilliant blue sapphire stone. The other was a band with several matching, but smaller, stones. The rings lay in her hand winking and glittering in the late evening light.

Memories sifted into her mind, vague and indistinct. She had hidden them here because, because—the reason seemed to evade her. The rings were synonymous with her marriage. Someone had tried to take them from her and she could not give them up because she didn't want to lose her husband—her marriage. But who had tried to take them from her? Her head had begun to ache. She strove to remember.

She never knew how long she stood there trying to remember but she was vaguely conscious that the ambulance and doctor had come. There were dim, far-away voices and then she was aware that the ambulance and the doctor's car had gone. She was still standing there with the rings blinking in her outstretched hand when she heard Clay call her name.

For one second more she continued to look down at the rings in her hand when suddenly the reality hit her like a blow in the stomach. If Clay saw her with the rings in her hand it would seal her chances with him forever! She looked about wildly for a place to hide them but there was no place. It was too late to put them back in their old hiding place as she had replaced the stone and Clay's steps were approaching rapidly.

The clattering footsteps stopped and Linn saw Clay at the top of the short flight of steps, just above her. She surreptitiously slid the hand concealing the rings and handkerchief into her sweater pocket and stood waiting for him.

Clay leaped down the few steps and stood before her. His face was a cold mask. He spoke impassively. "Linn, Mother is very ill. This is my fault. I should not have subjected her to the strain it brought when I allowed you to stay here. I must ask you to leave at once. I do not want you to ever come here again. The Volks is yours. You can take it or leave it. George will take you to the bus station. I am going to the hospital now."

He turned to go. She had been unable to say a word. Now she found her tongue. "Clay, I am sorry about your mother." He turned back to face her. She felt she had to say something to clear herself with him. But what could she say? "I—I—" she lifted an imploring hand from her sweater pocket. There was a flash of fire and a faint tinkle. Linn froze. Clay bent and picked up the two circlets of platinum. He straightened, and the look he bent upon her was awful to see. She shrank away from him.

"Clay," she faltered, "I—I can explain."

"I'll bet you can! You lied to me! You have been lying all along. And I had almost begun to believe you after George came to me and pled your case."

Hope sprang into Linn's heart. "Please let me explain. I didn't lie. I didn't know until a few minutes ago where these were hidden. Please believe me! Then I suddenly began to remember and I—I" She faltered to a stop as he threw back his head and laughed, a bark of derision.

"Get out of my sight, you little lying, thieving hypocrite! If you are here when I get back, I won't be responsible for what happens." He threw her wedding band at her feet and pocketing the star sapphire turned on his heel and started up the steps.

Linn caught him by the sleeve, "Clay, please—"

He turned back and shook her off. Then an incredulous look crossed his face; his lips curled in scorn. "So, now you use your last trick. Linn Randolph, the one who never cries, is crying!"

Linn put her hand to her face. Her face was wet with tears. "Please let me explain, please," she implored the stone face before her.

He laughed again, ugly and bitter, and started up the

steps. She caught him by the arm. "Please, please—"

He turned savagely and pushed her roughly against the wall. "Take your dirty hands off of me." His face was white and violence glinted in his eyes. She dropped her eyes dumbly and listened as his steps crunched on the path. The car motor started and she heard him go spinning away down the drive like demons were after him.

Linn collapsed in a heap on the stone bench. Her heart felt it would burst with pain. Her breath came in gasps and she felt she could hardly breathe. Indeed, she didn't want to breathe. She wanted to die!

Then the sobs came. They tore at her body and shook her frame convulsively. The pain in her heart was terrible. He had sent her away again and this was final. There was no chance of reconciliation—all hope was gone. Her world was in desolation. So great was her pain of heart and agony that she did not know she was remembering—vividly—now! She was crying for the heartbreak of Linn Randolph now, and the Linn of three years ago. The two were merging into one and, as she wept convulsively, she was appalled at the Linn of yesterday and she wept for her.

Three years ago, Clay had told her they were through and Linn had fought him bitterly both physically and verbally. The scene was graphic in Linn's mind now. She had tried to tear his face, so great was her grief and fury. Only his strong arms had prevented it. Then she had torn him to shreds verbally. She had called him every vile, dirty word she could find. Linn cringed in shame at the memory. Then he had thrust her away hard and sprinted up the steps and driven away.

Linn's sobs were quieting now, as the past rolled through her mind like a film. She had not cried then. She had prided herself on being tough and never crying. She had cried many bitter tears when she was a child and they had never availed her anything so she had steeled herself to never succumb to that weakness again.

She was now no longer crying for Linn who had just lost her husband for good, but for the girl of yesterday who could not cry, who had no friends, and who did not have God to go to. For now Linn felt her Savior's love as it wrapped her up and engulfed her, not erasing the pain or even the tears, but a love that said, "I am with you, Linn. You are My child and I'll never leave you. Don't be afraid of the future." As Linn felt His comfort like a healing balm spread through her being, she thought, If only Linn of yesterday had known God's love!

The film of memory was rolling still. Linn had walked down to the water's edge after Clay had driven away. She had felt despair wash over her in waves of desolation. She had stood for some moments twisting her rings on her finger. And abruptly she had remembered Clay trying to make her give up the star sapphire engagement ring. I must hide it, she had thought, frantically. It seemed if she gave up the ring she would never have another chance with Clay. So she had gone back to the wall and hidden the ring under the loose stone that she had noticed some time before.

Then she had gone back to the water's edge. She had thought, If I were not so afraid I would jump in and end it all. But the thoughts of the water covering and choking her had filled her with fear.

She had turned away from the water then. It had been almost dark, just as it was now. A figure had suddenly appeared beside her. She had been very frightened because she had thought she was alone. The figure was dressed in a light trench coat, wore gloves and had a hat pulled low over its head. The face must have been covered with a mask because the features were indistinct and frightening. The figure had reached out a black-gloved hand and said in a low monotone; "Give me the blue sapphire ring."

Linn had been petrified with fear and had backed to the water's edge with the figure pressing close with hand outstretched. She had tried to speak but could not as she was so afraid. She had tripped and fallen—and that was all she remembered.

Linn sat up and looked out at the water. So that was how

she came to be in the boat with a bump on her head! But who had the figure been? And had she fallen into the boat or had the person placed her there and set her adrift?

It was getting quite dark now and she looked around and shivered. She still did not know some answers but she must get to the house and get packed. She must not be here when Clay returned.

At least I am getting my memory back and, after all, that is what I came here for, she thought.

She stood up, brushed the sand from her clothes and went to the water's edge to wash the tears away. She did not know that ever since Clay's departure a man's figure had stood not far away and had observed her every move. The figure followed her now, keeping to the shadows, as she walked to the house. The man was George. It had been his opinion that Linn had attempted suicide three years ago and he planned to prevent such a happening again. So it was with much relief that he saw her enter the house.

Thirty minutes later, Linn called George to tell him she was ready to leave.

20

After Clay left Linn, he drove like a crazy person for several miles along the winding river road. It seemed to relieve the wild turmoil of his mind to punish the car and hear the tortured tires scream around the curves. But finally he gained control of his mind somewhat and slowed down to a fast but more reasonable speed.

It shook him to realize how angry he had been for the first few minutes after seeing those rings fall from Linn's pocket. He had been so furious that she had deceived and lied to him that he had felt violent and murderous urges raging through his brain. He shuddered. He could have murdered—almost, anyway—in the fit of rage that had torn at him. The feeling came flooding back now as he thought upon them and he quickly checked them. He had never thought himself of violent nature but the intenseness of his feelings now frightened him. He breathed slowly and deeply several times.

Clay reached the hospital in record time. He jumped out of the car and walked rapidly into the hospital. He didn't realize his feelings were mirrored in his face until Bonnie met him in the lobby and exclaimed, "Clay, whatever is the matter? Your face is as white as death and you look ready to murder someone!"

Clay forced himself to relax. This was something he didn't wish to discuss with anyone. Ignoring the question he asked, "How is Mother?"

"They have just taken her into 'emergency' but the doctor said you should take care of the entrance paperwork because she will be staying at the hospital."

Bonnie was of immeasurable help the next twenty-four hours. She was a step before him, or right behind, or beside him, whatever the need was. She cheered him, carried coffee and sandwiches to him, and he was glad to have her there. For one thing she took his mind from those last few stormy minutes with Linn that he was trying hard to forget.

His mother was kept sedated so heavily the first couple of days that Clay was not able to converse with her, but he stayed near her in case she called for him.

Eric was taking care of the home office to relieve Clay. Eric relayed the message from George that Linn was gone, by way of bus. She had taken only what she had brought and had left the little car behind.

When Eric conveyed this message from George, Clay felt an unaccountable intense feeling of loss. Linn was gone from his life. Why should he feel anything but relief? Visions of those poignant last few minutes with Linn crowded into his memory, unsummoned and distressing. He could see her face as she had clung to his arm, tears running down her face. The vision was so fresh in his memory that he felt almost as if someone else in the small waiting room near his mother's room might see it too. Suddenly he felt he had to get out, away from the persons in the room, away from Bonnie.

Muttering a few words of explanation, and rather abruptly refusing Bonnie's offer to accompany him, he hurried from the building. He walked to the corner and across the street to a small park. It was deserted except for a mother and her two small children down at the far end of the park where there were swings and a slide.

Clay sat down on a hard park bench to reflect. The poignant picture of Linn reasserted itself into Clay's memory. This time he let it stay. He had been closing his mind to any thought of Linn for two days. He would get her out in the open so he could deal with her and he hoped to forget her. As if that were possible!

As Clay allowed the picture of Linn to rise in his mind again, he suddenly realized his wild anger toward her had subsided. In its place was an ache so deep that it was a physical thing. Pictures of Linn, some laughing, some serious, and the powerful one of her crying, that kept returning to his consciousness, flitted through his memory. The pain was a wound of betrayal. He had loved her deeply, and had begun to trust her again and she had let him down. She had lied to him, deceived him, and at the same time insidiously coiled herself into his very being. The thought of her was pain, but his very being felt charged and exhilarated when he thought of her. Crazy, unthinkable and yet true! He loved her yet, even though she had utterly betrayed him!

Aghast at the duplicity of his own heart, Clay groaned in frustration. He got to his feet, to pace the length of the park.

Bonnie deserved better than this! She had not married when he had practically left her at the altar better than three years ago. Now here she was in almost the same position, only this time almost married to him who had a wife. Bonnie the faithful, always there when he needed her, standing by him as she was now. Beautiful, wealthy, sophisticated, a crown on anyone's head, and his deceitful heart said, "I love Linn! Linn—poor, mixed-up Linn!"

His feelings for Linn were deep and unfathomable. She was not as beautiful as Bonnie, but at the thoughts of her he felt his heart pound with intense feeling. The thoughts of her betrayal cut deep but he still loved her.

He returned to the hospital, but all through the day he was stabbed with thoughts of Linn. What had she done when she left Grey Oaks? He hoped she hadn't done anything foolish. Suicide? The thought sent him to his feet and he started to the door. Bonnie was at his side in a moment.

"Clay! What's the matter?"

Pulled up short, Clay knew how foolish his real explanation would be, so he prefabricated quickly. "I forgot to call home. The Grays will be looking for me to call."

Bonnie drew him back down to the couch. "Clay, dear, I have called twice a day and kept them informed. So relax."

Clay looked at Bonnie—at her stunning beauty. It was not fair for him to hold her longer. He could not marry her, feeling as he did for Linn. It would not be fair to Bonnie. He reached over and took both of her white, shapely hands. He saw the melting look in the violet depths of her dark eyes and winced.

"Bonnie," he began haltingly. "You have been a dear friend to me. I admire you tremendously and I'm flattered that you could care a hoot about me. But I can't marry you. It would not be fair to marry you when I still love Linn. I'm handling this like a lout, I know, but—"

Bonnie had pulled her hands away and was staring at him speechless. "You can't mean that! You are tired and distraught because of your mother!" Incredulity, anger, and shock registered in her face.

Suddenly Bonnie seemed to shake herself. She spoke softly. "This is no time to talk of such things. Let's drop it for now and later, when things are back to normal, we can have our little chat. Now, let's go see how your mother is faring."

And so the matter was shelved adroitly, leaving Clay feeling unsettled and unhappy. He was one who liked to have things tied in neat little packages with no loose ends dangling.

Mrs. Randolph had slept the whole night through. She awoke the next morning to find Clay dozing in the chair near her bed. She watched him for some time in silence. There was a brooding, contemplation in her eyes. A conflict began to show in those tired gray eyes, and pain, though not physical, caused tears to come. She twisted in bed and, turning her back to her son, silently wept.

21

A little later Bonnie arrived at the door and urged Clay to go out for some breakfast. She promised to stay with Mrs. Randolph while he was gone. This was a little unusual because her main concern was usually for him, but Clay asked no questions since he wanted to be alone. He went, promising to be back within an hour. He had some calls he had to make, also.

Bonnie busied herself with the flowers in the sick room, pinching off dead leaves and changing the water. Then she came back to sit next to Mrs. Randolph. Except for acknowledging Bonnie's presence when she had entered the room, Mrs. Randolph had lain quietly, with her eyes closed. She seemed to be asleep.

Bonnie leaned toward Mrs. Randolph and spoke softly but urgently. "Ethel, you must help me."

Clay's mother opened her eyes but said nothing.

Bonnie fixed her obsidian eyes upon the sick woman, laid a jeweled hand upon her arm and spoke imploringly, "Ethel, Clay imagines he is still in love with Linn. After all he believes her to be! It's ridiculous and absurd, but that is what he told me. He doesn't think it is fair to marry me when he still loves Linn!"

Mrs. Randolph still did not say anything or show any emotion. Bonnie's hand tightened on her arm and shook it slightly.

"We have got to plan what to do!" she exclaimed. "Clay is mine and I won't give him up to that—that little tramp."

Clay's mother's eyes widened and she spoke softly, "You are the one with all the tricks up your sleeve. Pull one out and use it. As for me, I am through with the whole matter!" She closed her eyes.

Angry fire leaped into Bonnie's eyes. "You are in this as deep as I am," she exploded, "and don't you forget it!" '

Ethel's eyes fluttered open and, for a brief second, fear showed in her eyes. Then it smoothed away and weary eyelids once more covered her gray eyes.

"Ethel!" The sharply spoken word was a command for attention. "If Clay found out what you have done, he would never forgive you. This was my idea, to be sure, but you sure grabbed at the chance to get that stupid girl out of Clay's life. Could you bear having Clay hate you for wrecking his marriage? Clay would hate you!" The words hung in the air like a coiled snake.

The coiled snake struck home, Bonnie observed triumphantly as she saw the ill woman's right hand clutch at her chest as if in pain and a long convulsive shudder shake her body. She laid so still that for a long suspenseful moment, Bonnie wondered if Ethel was dead. Then the woman opened her eyes and spoke.

"Bonnie, have you ever thought you were going to die?" She went on without waiting for an answer. "I almost died when I had that heart attack three days ago. I almost died and went to meet God three days ago!" She seemed to forget there was anyone else in the room, but continued in an odd agitated voice that tingled down Bonnie's backbone.

"Many years ago when I was a teenager, I attended church and learned about God, His Word and His Son, the

Lord Jesus Christ. But somehow I drifted away and haven't thought about him in years. Then Linn came back to Grey Oaks with God shining out of her eyes. Every time I look at her, it is God accusing me for the heinous wrong that I have done. Then when I almost died, I called out to God and He wasn't there!" The voice had risen only a little but it held terror and dread in the anguished words. "I can't find Him. What if I die and—and—" The woman covered her face with her hands and cried, "I'm afraid."

Bonnie, usually the poised, "in-command-of-any-situation" person, was more shaken than she would have liked to admit. However, she pulled herself together and spoke scoffingly.

"Ethel! Don't be melodramatic! I can't bear sentimental, religious people. This isn't like you. Now," she spoke with businesslike vigor, "I know we can handle this and it shouldn't even hurt your tender conscience. Clay has already sent Linn away, so all you have to do is tell him that he must promise to go ahead and marry me, just as we had planned, or it will just break your heart. Clay won't deny you anything while you are so ill." Her voice had become honeyed. "It was your desire that I marry Clay and you always detested Linn. I will make Clay happy, I can promise you that. I love him, Ethel! You will do it, won't you? This is for Clay's own good, and his happiness is what we both want more than anything else in life."

Mrs. Randolph took her hands from her face and spoke in a soft but decisive way. "No, I won't."

Bonnie was shocked. This was not the Ethel she knew, not the familiar Ethel that she could cajole or threaten into any plan that she, Bonnie, proposed. Well then! This would call for stronger measures, stronger weapons.

Bonnie bent close to Clay's mother, her words venomous. "Remember that I still have that note! That note and the interest it has accumulated would wreck Clay. He would have to take bankruptcy! You would both have to move out of luxury into poverty. Clay would have to start at the bottom. Clay, who has never known the stink and humiliation of poverty as you have. Grinding poverty! And with a blot on his name because he could not pay his honest debts. Think what you will do to your son, Mrs. Randolph!"

She sat back and watched with satisfaction the pallor that spread over the woman's features, the nervous flutter of the pale hands as they plucked at the lace of her expensive gown.

Ethel's voice was a wasted thin thread when she spoke. "You wouldn't do that to Clay! Not if you love him?"

Bonnie rose haughtily to her full diminutive, queenly height. "Just try me and see! Now, dear Ethel, I must leave you to reflect upon the cost to you and to Clay if you don't do this one small favor." She waited only long enough to see Ethel wearily close her eyes and note the tears as they ran down her cheeks to leave a dark stain on the spotless white of the hospital pillow. Then she walked out with a smug, satisfied expression on her lovely face.

22

When Clay returned a few minutes later, Bonnie told him that his mother was resting peacefully and now that he had returned, she would run downtown to do a little shopping that must be done.

"I'll be back in an hour or so," she said sweetly.

As Clay started into his mother's room, the head nurse came hurrying down the hall, calling out to him. She motioned Clay away from his mother's door and down the hall a few steps before speaking.

"Mr. Randolph, I hesitate to speak of this but I must because your mother's welfare is our greatest concern right now."

"Why, of course, Mrs Cantrol, what is the problem?" asked Clay, completely mystified.

"That young lady that is here at the hospital with you most of the time—"

"Oh, yes, you mean Bonnie. She is a close friend of our family."

"Well," the nurse went on, "when she left Mrs. Randolph's room a while ago, I went in to check on her and your mother was obviously very upset. She was crying and was as white as a sheet. Fortunately, her heart is still functioning normally but this sort of thing could be fatal to your mother. The doctor said she was to have absolutely no excitement. I'm afraid we must bar your young lady friend from our patient's room while she is so ill. You do understand, Mr. Randolph?"

"Of course, whatever you say. But she and Mother always get along so well I can't imagine what could have been said to upset her. Mom is like a mother to Bonnie. Can I go in to see her?"

"Yes, but please refrain from upsetting her in any way."

When Clay entered the room, he first thought his mother was sound asleep. She lay quiet and still. He tiptoed to her bedside. She was, indeed, very pale and there were traces of tears still upon her face. As he stood looking at her, she suddenly opened her eyes.

"Clay," she spoke in a weak, agitated voice, "I must talk to you. Please sit here right beside me so I won't have to speak very loud."

Clay put a finger gently upon her lips. "Mother, the nurse said you must not be upset or it could be dangerous to your heart. I'm sure, sweetheart, that whatever you have to say will keep until you are stronger. And I'll not be far at any time and will lend a willing ear after you get some more rest."

"No! No! I must tell you now! I can't rest until I tell you."

Clay was becoming alarmed. He remonstrated with her. "Please, Mom, calm down. There is nothing more important than getting well. Go to sleep now and I promise to stay right here, and if you are stronger when you wake up I will be glad to listen. Shall I have the nurse give you something to help you sleep?"

"No! I refuse to go to sleep until I talk to you! It must be done now while I still have the courage!" Her voice sounded stronger now, but distraught.

"Very well, fire away. But make it brief because I'll be banned from visiting rights if that nurse hears you carrying on like this. Please calm down first. And speak slowly and low so you won't exert yourself."

Clay took a chair at her side and waited.

Mrs. Randolph made a visible effort to calm down. She closed her eyes and took several slow even breaths. When she spoke again her voice was controlled and low. She closed her eyes.

"I hardly know where to begin or how to tell you what I have done . . . When I was a little girl and into my teens I never knew anything but the direst of poverty. Dad was the town drunk and I saw Mother slowly wither away and die, partly from hardship and hard work but a lot from a broken heart, I think. But when I was in high school I met Ruth, Bonnie's mother. She had everything I didn't have and I will never know why she chose me for her friend. She was an only child of loving wealthy parents. Perhaps she felt sorry for me in the beginning, but we became warm, inseparable friends. Before long, her parents asked me to live with them, and I did. They sent me to college with their own daughter and dressed me in the best and gave me spending money as if I were their own child. This was what Ruth wanted, and Ruth's wish was their command. And never once in all the years of our friendship did Ruth ever treat me as anything but an equal and a dear friend. She never made me feel dependent and would never even let me thank her properly, though I often tried."

She paused for a moment and breathed heavily before continuing.

"The good things of life always came through her, it seemed. She even introduced me to your father. When we were out of college and married to two fine young men, who were best friends also, we were still very close.

"When I gave birth to a son and six months later Ruth bore a girl, we began to joke about you two growing up and marrying. At first it was in fun, but long before you two were grown it became our fervent wish that you two would feel the same way. We gave you as much time together as we deemed wise and it was a dream come true to Ruth and me when you and Bonnie announced your engagement in your senior year at college. I was always glad that Ruth did not die before she knew of your plans.

"So it came as a cruel shock to me, Clay," she continued, "when just a few months out of college and a few months short of your wedding to Bonnie, you met Linn and in a month's time you had broken your engagement to Bonnie and had married Linn.

"I didn't like Linn from the start, but I suppose that I would not have liked anyone who tried to usurp what I felt was Bonnie's rightful place."

Ethel seemed relaxed and almost as if she were talking to herself so Clay leaned back in his chair and listened to this enlightening account. Clay had never known his mother to speak of her past and he wondered idly now why he had never been curious.

"I never went out of my way to make Linn like me. In fact, I am sure I tried in little ways to make her feel like the interloper I felt she was. But overall, the first few months of your marriage I didn't behave too badly. And then your father died. In my hurt and loneliness, perhaps I wanted to take it out on someone. Your father had always liked Linn and defended her against any criticism. I had resented that."

Clay nodded, as though he remembered well what she was saying.

"Bonnie came to the funeral. Ruth was dead by now and we were both lonely so I began to go out to eat with Bonnie or invite her to our home. Somewhere in those first few meetings we began to brew a plan to get rid of Linn. I was seething with resentment against Linn. I didn't like her fiery temper or her outspokenness. Some of my complaints were real, because Linn didn't care for me either, and didn't try to conceal the fact. But many were imaginary. Bonnie still wanted to marry you. She had always loved you, she said."

Clay was sitting tense now, his face set.

"We knew your marriage was rocky, because you were both high-tempered and strong-willed. So Bonnie devised a plan to make Linn jealous. She would accidentally run into you here and there and either wrangle an invitation for coffee or invite you to have lunch with her. With the help of friends she would see to it that Linn knew about it. She made it appear that you were meeting purposely behind Linn's back. Of course you never suspected any of this because Bonnie was a friend of the family and it only seemed natural to have coffee or lunch together if you 'happened' to run into each other. But you can remember, I am sure, what a row those 'happenstances' caused."

Clay could scarcely believe his mother's persistence in relating these facts to him. It was as though she had to get it all out in the open.

"But this was not enough to cause a permanent break between you" she went on "so we cast about for something else to use. I thought I was quite clever when I hit upon the plan to call the orphanage to see if Linn had any outstanding problem when she lived there. When I found she had briefly stolen things, we knew we had found the perfect tool. So we planted things in her room, and even in her clothes, to make her look like a disturbed compulsive thief." Ethel's voice sank almost to a whisper. "Then when you were at the end of your rope with a stormy, uncooperative wife—you had begged her to accept psychiatric help—I staged a heart attack. And that finished your patience with Linn. You broke with her."

There was complete silence for a time. Clay was trying to absorb it all; his mother was trying to control her emotions.

"Of course my conscience has tormented me much the

three years Linn was gone and believed drowned but I always rationalized that she was a scheming golddigger and it was best for all of us that she was gone."

A shuddering sob ran through her form and she struggled to control it. Clay's face was ashen and he sat staring at her as though mesmerized. With obvious great effort she drew a long sigh and continued.

"But when Linn returned, she was not the same Linn. I knew immediately what caused that change. Many years ago, as a child and young teenager, I attended Sunday School and church regularly, prayed and read my Bible religiously. Although I never made a personal commitment to Christ, I knew many in our small church who had an experience like Linn has. I never talked to you about the Lord, Clay, because by the time you were born I had set Ruth up in God's place. She was the source of the good things of life for me. I never realized until these past three days of soul-searching that God was the one who sent Ruth my way and caused her to befriend me when I was no more to her than anyone else in that high school. God had answered my prayers for a better life and I did what the heathen of old have done. I worshiped at the feet of the created instead of the Creator."

Clay looked at his mother in amazement, but kept his silence.

"Clay, I have been in torment these past few weeks. I never saw the hideousness, the callousness, the cruelty of what I have done until Linn came back and I had to meet and account to God every day, and there was no good excuse or reason, when I met God every day in Linn's face. Clay have you noticed it?"

Clay nodded slowly, "Yes, Mom, I have."

"At first Bonnie did most of the dirty work. You know the obsession she has for wearing the family star sapphire ring. She searched Linn's suitcases but failed to find it. Then she set out to drive Linn away. She used every scare tactic in the book: threats, poison oak, that crazy ride down Whitebird Mountain, and even stalked her on the beach after dark.

When nothing succeeded, and she saw you down by the river almost kiss Linn, she almost went berserk. In desperation she resorted to the old kleptomania deception and prevailed upon me to help. I hid the necklace and tie clip in Linn's room. Later, when I saw George go to your room, I followed and heard him defending Linn and telling you what a changed person she was. I couldn't sleep at all that night. I was tangled in a web of deceit from which there seemed no escape and remorse was tearing me to shreds.

Clay was beginning to feel sick inside as his mind raced to recall the incidents she recounted. He grew pale.

"Then to make matters worse," Ethel went on, "Bonnie forced me back into the old sordid deception. I would not do it at first, but she produced a paper—a note—that said your father owed her father and had never repaid. If it is a real note, it could bankrupt you. She threatened to foreclose on it but said if I would help her she would tear up the note."

"I had not been able to find peace night or day until it was too much for my weak heart. When I had that heart attack three days ago, it came to me with great force that if I died in this condition, and did not make things right, I would be forever and eternally lost."

Ethel's voice was very low and weak now, spent with the effort and the emotional strain the telling of her story had wrought.

She paused, and Clay tried to speak but she went on, "I have tried to find the God of my youth and He has hidden His face from me. Clay, I almost died—without God! And —I—was—afraid! So afraid!" She covered her face with trembling hands and began to cry.

23

Clay sat as one turned to stone. He knew he should comfort his mother, try to calm her or it could be disastrous to her weakened heart, but his whole body seemed numb—

cold, and incapable of movement or voice. His head had a humming sensation inside, and for a brief moment the room tilted and righted itself, then tilted and spun around, and his mother's quiet sobs seemed far away.

Then his head began to clear and burning rage took its place—rage at his mother, at Bonnie, at himself. The horror of the whole heinous deception and what it had done to Linn, and to himself, swept over him and he felt that he wanted to slash and hurt and cause cruel pain to those who had done this thing. The intensity of his feelings frightened him, and he struggled to his feet. He must get out of here. At the moment he hated his mother with a burning passion. He must get out of here!

He rushed from the room, half running down the corridor. He took the stairs down to the lower level. The walls were pressing in upon him and he felt he was suffocating. He dashed downward two steps at a time like demons were pursuing him.

He pushed out into the hall, through the entrance lobby and almost ran into Bonnie coming into the hospital. She started to speak, but with one look at his ashen face and eyes burning with a strange frightening fire, the words died on her lips. When his eyes lit on her, she drew back as though afraid he was going to strike her. Then his lips curled in contempt and he said through clinched teeth, "Get out of my sight while I can still restrain myself."

Bonnie turned and fled away from him, down the hospital hall. Clay charged on out into the balmy, sunny day. He walked swiftly away from the hospital, not heeding nor caring where he was going.

The pace he set was grueling but he kept it up for hours, trying to escape the visions tumbling through his tortured brain. He tried not to think of those last few minutes he had been with Linn and the anguish and pain she must have felt—the tears running down her face, her pleading with him and the words he had said. But it was all there in his brain like indelible fire, burning and searing his very soul.

He remembered now, vividly, all the times he had doubted her before she had been driven away the first time, and now it had all happened again. No wonder his heart had refused to forget Linn. It seemed to know what his brain had not known. Linn was innocent and always had been! The thought should have brought joy, but it could only bring searing, agonizing, self-condemnation.

Had he known his own wife so little that he could not trust and defend her against all deprecation? At first, he remembered, he could not believe she would steal or lie. Jealousy, yes, he could believe that of the other Linn. But gradually they had worn away his confidence with what appeared to be undeniable proofs.

His teeth ground together in helpless fury. Bonnie and his mother had planned so well it all had been so convincing. It was understandable that he had finally succumbed to their devious plot. But how could he have been so dumb? Just plain dumb! Linn was his wife! If anyone should have known her through and through, he, her husband, should have. It was inexcusable! And so the battle raged in his mind and inner being.

He felt a raging anger against Bonnie and his poor weak mother but he especially loathed himself. He could flee away from the other two who had caused Linn unspeakable wrong but from himself he could not escape.

He walked until his legs nearly collapsed. He saw that he was at the edge of town, near a woods. He must have been walking all around inside the small town because he knew he had walked for several hours. He entered the stand of trees and presently found a small clearing. He sank down upon the grass and laid back upon the ground. His body and mind felt bruised and beaten. His legs ached. With great effort he tried to clear his mind and think what must be done. The very act of lying so still in the peacefulness of the heavy pines seemed to have a calming effect. His mind began to clear.

He told himself that he must stop behaving like an idiot and think the thing through rationally. It helped. He must find

Linn as quickly as possible. Valuable time had already been lost. He must try to get her to forgive him and if she would forgive and be willing to begin again, he would spend the rest of his life making up to her what he and Bonnie and his mother had done to her.

His mother! He realized with a stab in his heart that he had completely forgotten about her. She had done a terrible thing to him, and to Linn, but she was still his mother and he was responsible for her. He grudgingly conceded in his mind that it had taken real courage for her to tell the truth. He also realized with a pang that he did not really know his own mother. He had never known her to have a concern for God or what God thought. She was not a churchgoer at all. She had never talked about God or mentioned God to him in his whole life, not even when he was a child. He knew that some mothers, even non-Christians, taught their children little nighttime prayers and mealtime prayers, but his mother never had. How strange that she had once apparently been a regular churchgoer, and she had never spoken to her own child about God.

In fact, he didn't really know Bonnie, either—Bonnie, his friend of a lifetime. Once he had thought he knew her well and had real affection for her—and he thought he loved her. And it was this person who had perpetrated this cruelest of hoaxes upon himself and Linn!

His blood began to boil again and he quickly shifted his mind to thoughts of his mother. He must get back to the hospital. His mother needed him. Could he forgive her enough to at least go through the actions of a devoted son to help her get well? Her whole life was wrapped up in him, and without his support at this time she could well give up and die.

Did he hate his mother? He did not know. His feelings were too unstable at present to form a rational conclusion. He certainly felt no love for her right now—or even compassion. He realized that if it wouldn't kill her he would like her to feel cruel mental pain and anguish. It would serve her right for what she had subjected Linn to!

But he must not go on in this vein of thinking. He had a responsibility to his mother, if for no other reason, for the fact that she was his mother and he was all she had. He must get back to her.

As he neared his mother's room, the head nurse hurried to meet him. "Mr. Randolph, I want you to please speak to the young lady that you called Bonnie. Right after you left, she came back to see your mother. My back was turned for just a moment and she went in. I saw her when she came out and asked her not to visit anymore until your mother was stronger. She replied that she would visit whenever she pleased. Then I went into the room and found your mother in a very distraught condition."

Clay nodded, "I'll see what I can do." But the nurse was persistent.

"I'm so glad you are here. She keeps asking for you and she has refused to take anything to quiet her nerves. I have been trying to reach the doctor to get permission to give her a shot whether she wants it or not."

As Clay pushed past her and walked into the room, he was horrified to feel a flash of pleasure in the fact that his mother was apparently doing a little suffering of her own. Quickly he suppressed this traitorous feeling and as the nurse watched anxiously, advanced to Mrs. Randolph's side.

His mother looked bad. Her face was lined and haggard-looking. He thought with a sudden burst of feeling, Why, Mother is getting old! Ethel's eyes were still closed, so he closed his own eyes and tried to conjure up a vision of his mother as old and tired and in need of what help he could give her. It helped him to feel compassion a moment later when she spoke his name.

Her voice was weak and she was definitely upset. She asked the nurse if she could be alone with Clay for a few minutes. When the nurse began to remonstrate, she promised to take anything or do anything the nurse asked if she could only speak with Clay privately first. The nurse acquiesced but told her she must be brief.

As soon as they were alone, Mrs. Randolph cried out, "Bonnie was here and she said she had made a promise to Linn that if Linn broke up you and Bonnie that she would make her sorry that she was ever born! I think she plans to harm Linn to get even with you, and me too, I suppose. Clay, you must do something!"

"Isn't it a little late for you to be concerned as to what happens to Linn?" Clay's voice was cold and cutting. In spite of all his good intentions, Clay's feelings had surfaced. He could have bitten his tongue at the expression in her eyes.

"You are right, Clay. Hurt me any way you feel like and it will not undo the harm I have done. I have it coming." Her words were humble and sincere.

"But that does not alter the fact that your wife could be in grave danger. I know Bonnie better than you. You have never seen her claws. They can be very wicked if they are turned on you. She could be bluffing, or just angry, but I wouldn't count on it."

"Mother, I am sorry. That remark was unnecessary. And I do appreciate your concern. If you feel you will be okay by yourself for a few hours, I will fly up to Aliceville and see Linn. She is okay, I am sure, or the doctor would have called us. So don't worry about a thing and I'll be back in a few hours. I plan to have a private nurse with you from now on when I'm not here so don't worry that Bonnie will bother you again. Remember that you promised the nurse to be a good girl and go to sleep."

Mrs. Randolph searched her son's face for a moment and then closed her eyes. "I promised and I will. Tell Linn that I am very sorry. She will never know how very sorry. Now, I must sleep. I am very tired." Her voice trailed off and her breathing became regular and even. The lines seemed to ease from her face and Clay realized that she had now put things in his hands and she meant to rest them there.

24

Clay went softly from the room and made quick arrangements for a private nurse. He left specific orders that no one, and especially Bonnie, should be allowed into Mrs. Randolph's room. He waited until the special nurse arrived and gave the orders again.

Then Clay drove rapidly to the airport, rented a plane, and in an hour was in Aliceville knocking at the door of Doctor Andrew Glover.

Mrs. Glover answered the knock. She was a pretty, slim, sweet-faced woman with short gray hair curling girlishly about her face.

"I would like to speak with Linn Randolph," Clay said. "Is she here or at the doctor's office?"

Mrs. Glover said with no hesitation, "I'm sorry, but Linn is out of town for a few weeks. May I help you in some way?"

Disappointment rose like a dark wave in Clay's heart. "I am Clay Randolph, Linn's husband. Could you tell me where she has gone?"

"I don't understand," Mrs. Randolph was obviously puzzled. "Isn't Linn still with you?"

Panic made Clay's knees go weak and he found himself floundering in tangled-up words as he tried to explain everything and ask questions at the same time. Then he steadied himself and began again. "I won't go into everything but things haven't been going well at my house for several days. They came to a climax three days ago when my mother had a serious heart attack. I felt Linn was responsible so I sent her away. I presumed she would come back here. Today I found out some things that make it imperative that I see Linn right away."

Mrs. Glover's face paled and she put out a hand to the doorway to steady herself. "Linn has not called us for several days. We have been concerned but she never intimated that things weren't going well."

She took a deep breath and went on before Clay could speak again. "What state was she in when you saw her last?" She rushed on before he could answer. "Linn was in a terrible mental state when she came to us three years ago. Her nerves were in a complete state of collapse. Something, or someone, had driven that child almost out of her mind. If someone has done this thing to her again I feel that I could— could—" She broke off and demanded fiercely, "Was she okay when you saw her last?"

Clay felt fear stab his inner being. He had been afraid that Bonnie might harm Linn but this was a new fear and a more dreadful one to consider. Oh, what had he done to Linn! He very well knew why Linn had arrived here in that terrible state. He and his mother and Bonnie had driven her there. But where was Linn now? He had to find her. He had to and he hoped he would not be too late.

He had forgotten Mrs. Glover for the moment.

He came out of his reverie because someone was shaking his arm. He looked up and Mrs. Glover was asking urgently, "Was Linn okay when you saw her last? Please tell me!"

Clay shook his head to clear it and considered before he answered slowly, "I don't know. I hope so. She was crying. I was very angry and when I drove away she was still standing down near the river." His voice broke, "You don't think she would take her own life?" He said aghast.

Tears were running down Mrs. Glover's face but she seemed unaware of them. "We must call Andrew." Suddenly she let out a glad cry. "Thank God, there he is now!" A small gray car coasted to a stop in the tree-shaded drive and Dr. Glover climbed stiffly out and came along the walk.

Without preamble, Mrs. Glover rushed to the crux of the matter. "Andrew, Linn left the Randolph's three days ago and they don't know where she is."

Alarm showed briefly in the doctor's face and then he

was the doctor again, used to emergencies of all kinds. "Come on into the house and let's talk where the neighbors can't hear us. Mona, could you get us some coffee?"

When they were in the living room, Dr. Glover leaned back and spoke calmly, "Now, young man, tell us about Linn."

Clay found that Dr. Glover had put him at ease, at least as much as was possible under the circumstances.

"Doctor, Mrs. Glover said Linn has not called you for several days. She hasn't contacted you in any way?"

"None, whatsoever. We were considering calling her tonight if she hadn't called us. Linn is very close to us. We never had any children and Linn has become like our own," he said in simple explanation. "You say she left your house three days ago? This is certainly not like Linn to leave without letting us know. What happened that she left so suddenly?"

All at once Clay had a desire to tell these people everything. "If you will bear with me I will tell you as briefly as possible the whole story."

"Please do," the doctor said and his wife nodded her head in agreement.

Clay took a sip of the hot coffee and began.

"I met Linn at one of our branch real estate offices where she was working. We had a whirlwind courtship and were married within three weeks. My father liked Linn from the first but Mother did not. You see, I had been engaged to marry Bonnie Leeds, the daughter of Mother's closest friend, for two years. We had known each other all of our lives and it was the fondest hope of the two mothers that we would marry. Everyone expected we would marry and I never seriously considered marrying anyone else until I met Linn.

"Things went fairly smoothly, until my father and Bonnie's mother died within a few weeks of each other. Bonnie and Mother turned to each other for consolation. Bonnie began to spend a great deal of time at our house. Linn was naturally quite jealous of her. Bonnie is a beautiful woman. Linn and I began to have violent quarrels about

Bonnie.

"I did not know until today that Mother and Bonnie planned and schemed ways to use Linn's jealousy to break us up. But though we did have some vicious arguments we always made up.

"My mother just told me about their plots, today. When the jealousy manuever failed, they hatched up a diabolical plan to discredit Linn. They hid articles of all kinds, even some that were taken from our guests, in Linn's room and cleverly made her to appear to be a kleptomaniac."

Mrs. Glover gasped but her husband laid his hand gently on her arm and motioned Clay to continue.

"At first I couldn't, and wouldn't, beleve the evidence. But gradually they wore me down. At that time Linn had a violent temper and we quarreled more and more frequently and violently. I urged her to get professional help and, of course, she declared she needed no help and stormed that my household was trying to turn me against her. I had never known Mother to lie, so I finally sided solidly against Linn. Then, to climax the whole thing, my mother faked a very convincing heart attack. I think it wasn't too hard because by this time she was thoroughly sick of the whole sordid mess but Bonnie wouldn't let her out. Bonnie claimed she held a note that would ruin me financially if Mother didn't continue to lend her support. There was such a note but I have a receipt to prove it was paid long ago but Mother didn't know this.

"Anyway, when Mother collapsed, I violently quarreled with Linn and told her we were through. I felt Linn had caused Mother's heart attack with her erratic behavior and the embarrassment it had caused us all. I demanded back the star sapphire engagement ring that is a family heirloom. Linn said it would be over her dead body. I was so angry that I left Linn quickly. I felt I could even harm her, I was so angry.

"That's the last anyone of our household saw of Linn until she came with you a while back. We felt she had committed suicide. We searched for her, of course, but the evidence seemed so strong and Linn was so emotional, we felt that was the only explanation."

Clay sat motionless for a moment as if drained by the effort it had taken to tell the story. Then he began again in a strained voice.

"I was furious when Linn came back on the scene. I felt the amnesia story was just another lie. I was engaged again to marry Bonnie. But as I was thrown together with Linn more and more the past three weeks, I began to see she was different and I realized before long that I loved Linn just as much as ever. I began to hope that we could be together again as we were in the early months of our marriage.

"And then things began to come up missing again, just as before. Things moved rapidly from that. Of course Linn denied everything. She didn't storm and rant, as she did before, but all the old scenes came alive in my memory. And then three days ago Mother collapsed with a heart attack— this time a real one. I found Linn right away, as soon as we had Mother in the ambulance and on the way to the hospital.

"I was intent on breaking with her for good. Linn was down by the river. Giving her no chance to speak, I told her she was the reason for Mother's heart attack and ordered her to leave Grey Oaks and never return. Trying to reason with me, she stretched out her hand to me and two rings fell from her pocket. Linn had told me she could not remember what had happened to them. One was the blue star sapphire engagement ring and the other was her wedding band.

"When I saw the rings I almost went berserk. I accused her of being a hypocrite and lying to me all along. She declared she had just remembered where they were. Of course in my distraught condition I didn't believe her. I'm afraid I got pretty ugly. I told her we were through forever and ordered her to be gone before I came back or suffer the consequences."

Clay's voice dropped to almost a whisper, and he had difficulty going on. "She came after me and pled with me, with tears running down her face." Clay choked and stopped.

He got up quickly and walked about the room trying to regain his composure. Finally, he went to stand before the window with his back to them and went on in a choked voice, "She reached out her hand and caught my arm. When I saw her tears, I—I saw red. I thought it was just another trick to gain my sympathy. I shoved her back against the wall." His voice choked off again for a moment, then he went on doggedly. "But I don't think I hurt her. When I got to the car and looked back she was still standing there, like she was stunned or—or something. That's the last time I saw her."

He turned back to face them. "That was three days ago. I have been at the hospital most of the time since Mother almost died from the heart attack. Guilt has been eating Mother up and she was afraid to die with that on her conscience, so she told me the whole story. I thought Linn would be here, so here I am. Now where do I look? I must find her," he said dramatically. She could even be in danger. Mother said that Bonnie threatened Linn that if she broke us up again, she would harm her—and I told Bonnie yesterday that I couldn't marry her because I still loved Linn, whatever Linn was. Bonnie tried to coerce Mother into getting me to change my mind. Mother is afraid Bonnie means to harm Linn."

The doctor spoke slowly. "Do you think that is what happened to Linn before? Remember, she came to us with a big lump on her head. By all rights she should have died in the rapids."

The color drained slowly from Clay's face. "Surely Bonnie didn't try to kill her. I can believe that she might try to frighten her—but to commit murder. It seems so—so preposterous."

The muscles in Dr. Glover's jaw tightened. "Anyone who would deliberately set out to wreck a marriage and, in the process, nearly drive a girl mad, would be capable of anything. Wouldn't you agree?"

Clay stared fixedly at the doctor for a moment. Then he reached over and grasped the doctor's arm in a tight grip.

"We've got to find her! You should know where she might go!"

"We'll all do all we can, of course, but we are at a loss to know where she might go as much as you. I would have thought, as you did, that she would have come here first. She knows we would be very concerned." The doctor stroked his chin in a reflective gesture. "I believe she will contact us, unless, of course—" He left the words dangling in the air. Clay pounced on them.

"Unless what?" he demanded.

The doctor seemed to shake himself mentally. "Let's not do any conjecturing. We'll call some friends of Linn's and inquire around. Mona, why don't you get some phone numbers ready. Clay, isn't there any place you can think of that she might have gone? No? Well, think on it a bit. You may come up with something."

The next hour was a busy one, spent calling friends and acquaintances. But the calls were all fruitless. No one had seen or heard from Linn. When all the posibilities had been checked out, Doctor Glover again urged Clay to do some earnest thinking.

"Think of where Linn went while she was at your house. Did she attend church? Did she—"

Clay interrupted him eagerly, "Sure, she went to a little church in town—at least once that I know of and I believe more than that!"

The pastor of the small church was called but that also was a deadend street. The pastor was kind and wished to help. Yes, he remembered the young lady. She had filled out a visitor's card but had checked on the card that she did not want anyone to call. He had spoken briefly with her at the door the two times she had come, but no one else had visited with her even briefly as she had hurried away at the close of both services. He was sorry he could be of no help.

So they were back at the starting place. Each one sat and racked his brain but there seemed to be no other leads. Linn had been a rather shy girl and made few close friends.

Mrs. Glover brought in a light lunch and they discussed what to do further over coffee, sandwiches and salad.

Suddenly, Doctor Glover laid his sandwich down and looked across at his wife. "There is someone who knows where Linn is and we have completely overlooked Him."

A look of excitement instantly sprang into Clay's eyes and he leaned forward expectantly.

Dr. Glover glanced over at his young guest and spoke earnestly. "Mona and I have served God for many years and have seen Him do some remarkable things in the past. It is time we took this matter of Linn's disappearance to God in prayer."

Clay sat back. The animation went out of his face. His lip curled a bit disdainfully as he spoke stiffly. "I'm not a religious man myself, but if you two want to pray, go ahead." He dropped his eyes and waited.

Dr. Glover eyed the younger man with slight amusement and then bowed his head. Mrs. Glover prayed first, then her husband. Clay listened. Somehow he felt embarrassed and uncomfortable. They talked just as though God was in the room and as if they felt He heard every word and would do what they asked. Someway, the simplicity and sincerity of their prayers made Clay wish he were somewhere else. It didn't seem consistent with the obvious fact that they were educated, intelligent persons. The whole thing seemed so childish to his sophisticated mind. He was glad when their simple petition to God was over and they all could get back to the business of finding Linn.

Self-consciously, Clay finished his lunch. The Glovers did not seem a bit self-conscious about their actions, as if it were as natural as breathing to stop in the middle of a meal and talk to God as though they knew Him personally as a Friend who would be glad to assist them in locating Linn. The whole thing left Clay with an uneasy feeling and he couldn't for the life of him imagine why.

The phone rang as they were finishing lunch. Mrs. Glover answered and as she listened her face lit up and she became decidedly excited, though she spoke calmly.

"But where is she? Oh—Did she say when she would contact us? Yes—yes, I understand. Be sure and call us if you hear from her again. We have been quite concerned. And thank you very much for calling."

Clay sprang from his chair. "Where is she? That was about Linn, wasn't it?"

Mrs. Glover sat back down before she answered. "Yes, that was about Linn. But I still don't know where she is. Only that she is well and safe."

Clay leaned over the table with his hands flat on the table, tense as a spring. "Who called? They must tell us where she is! I must talk to her!"

Mrs. Glover spoke soothingly. "The call was from Mr. Trestle at the bank. Linn called and had him send her some money from her savings, and she also left a message for us." She turned to her husband. "She said to tell us not to worry. That she was well and she hoped we had not worried about her. She said she would get in touch with us later. She had some things she needed to take care of and she wanted the satisfaction of knowing she was capable of handling her own affairs again with no help from anyone except God. She said she loves us and not to worry."

Clay had listened to the message with bated breath. At the end he asked, "Did she mention anything about me or—or anything?"

Mrs. Glover spoke kindly but decisively. "No, she mentioned nothing at all of what took place at your home or between you two."

"I'm going over to see that Mr. Trestle," Clay declared. "I must find out where Linn is. I've got to see her, talk to her."

Dr. Glover shook his head slowly. "You can go, of course, but I'm afraid you are bound for disappointment.

Linn apparently doesn't want anyone knowing where she is right now and if such is the case I am afraid Glen Trestle would never divulge her whereabouts."

"It's worth a try, anyway," Clay stated determinedly.

But Dr. Glover was right in his surmise. Mr. Trestle did not have anything except a name of a town the money had been sent to, general delivery to the post office. He apologized profusely, but adamantly refused to disclose the name of the town where Linn was, or even the state. Clay implored him, telling him he was Linn's husband and that it was imperative that he contact Linn, but Mr. Trestle would not yield an inch. He did promise to tell Linn that Clay wished to speak with her, if she should call or write again. But he had no idea if she would call again. He also agreed to send a letter from Clay to the same town where she had asked the money to be sent. But he did not know if she would call for any mail there again.

So Clay had to be content for the present with placing a brief appeal in an envelope and leaving it in Mr. Trestle's hand.

25

The taxi slowed, turned a corner, and cruised slowly down a street lined with small shabby houses and apartments.

"There," the cab driver pointed, "That's the number you're looking for."

With a quick apprehensive glance at the tiny, dingy house the cabby indicated, Linn paid the driver and sent him on his way. Taking her two suitcases, Linn approached the house with quaking heart. If this were truly the current address, she was about to see the aunt that she had not seen since being placed in the orphanage many years ago.

How would she receive her? If this aunt had really cared

for her, would she have allowed Linn to go to an orphanage? Or, if it had been as Miss Forrest, the Children's Home Superintendent, had stated, the aunt had been in very poor health and had a new baby to raise, could she not have at least come to visit her?

All of these thoughts tumbled through her mind as Linn stood on the sidewalk in front of the humble abode. She wondered with a sinking heart if she should have come. Perhaps she should have called first. But, from the looks of the house, it was doubtful if the occupant could afford a telephone.

Should she even go in, now that she was here? Or was she just a coward? Indecision gripped her. She set the suitcases down and looked the place over critically. No sound came from within. But the whole aura of the pitiful little house was poverty: from the peeling paint, to the cracked sidewalk and scrap of hard-packed bare ground in front.

She had been so certain when she had earnestly prayed before leaving the Randolph mansion yesterday. As she prayed, she had suddenly thought of her aunt that she had not seen in so long and a great longing had risen in her heart to see her. She had tucked the address in her purse when Miss Forrest at the orphanage had given it to her. She had found it quickly and never had a doubt but that she should look her up—until now.

Suddenly, she had another thought. Linn, are you a snob? Do you shrink from contact with anyone in such poor circumstances? She examined this new thought and decided that it was possible. She had lived in comfortable, luxurious surroundings for a long time and it was true that she cringed at the thought of having to live, even briefly, in a place like this.

Well, that settled it! She would not allow herself to be turned aside from what had seemed to be God's leading by a flimsy excuse like that! So, picking up her suitcases and squaring her shoulders, Linn marched resolutely to the door.

But just as she raised her hand to knock, the door opened abruptly and a figure rushed out the door and collided with Linn, knocking the suitcases from her hands and nearly knocking the breath from her. Linn caught her balance before she completely fell and put out a steadying hand to the embarrassed and apologizing young girl who had so nearly run her down.

The girl was very blond, and thin to the point of skinniness. She seemed to be "all legs," like a young colt. Linn gasped as she looked into the pointed face and startled green eyes. She had no doubt that this was where her aunt lived. This child of perhaps ten or eleven years old was an exact, younger likeness of Linn herself.

The child had stopped her stammered apologizing and was regarding Linn with a quizzical expression.

"Do I know you?"

"Not really," Linn said with a sudden catch in her voice. "You see, we are cousins and we look much alike. Your mother is my aunt. Our mothers were sisters. Kate Linn Marshall is your mother's name, isn't it?"

The blond child continued to stare at Linn in fascination as if this was all too much to take in.

"Your mother's name is Kate Linn Marshall, isn't it?" Linn prodded gently. "Where is your mother?" she asked when she received no answer.

The last question seemed to snap the child from her mesmerism. Her face fell and she looked as if she might break into tears but controlled herself. "Yes, that's my mother's name. She's in there." She pointed disconsolately toward the house.

Puzzled, Linn asked, "Is something wrong?"

The child fixed grave green eyes upon Linn. "What's a foster home? The doctor just told Mother I was going to have to go to one for a while. Mother's trying to argue with him, but I don't guess it will do much good. She's sick and has to go to the hospital. The doctor says so. Only mother doesn't think she's that sick or so she's telling the doctor. But I'm afraid the doctor's right. Mother's really been sick for a long time but she wouldn't admit it to me. She knows I worry," she finished with a sigh.

Linn felt her heart give a lurch of pain. Had she found her only family, just to have them snatched away again? No, no! It couldn't be so. She wouldn't let it happen!

"Could we go in and see about this?" Linn tried to speak cheerfully over the pounding of her troubled, protesting heart.

Linn's cousin led the way into the sparsely furnished, but clean little living room. Voices from the next room came clearly through the thin walls, even though the door was shut.

"Mrs. Marshall, there is no other way. You do not seem to realize how very ill you are. You must go to the hospital. You do want to live to raise your daughter, don't you? I assure you that your little girl will be well cared for." The deep voice broke off as a weak voice answered so low that the two in the living room could not hear.

Linn felt a cold hand on her arm and she looked down into the tear-filled eyes of her young cousin. "Make her go to the hospital," she quavered. "She might di—die if she doesn't. I won't mind going to a foster home, really I won't, if Mother can only get well again."

Linn stared at that pale face and beseeching green eyes for another brief moment. Then, squeezing the child's hand comfortingly, she crossed to the closed door and knocked softly, pushing it open before she received an answer.

The doctor turned with an annoyed expression on his stern features which quickly changed to surprise. Linn moved swiftly to her aunt's side and took her thin (shockingly thin) hand into her own warm left hand while she extended her right to the doctor.

"Doctor, I am Linn Randolph, Mrs. Marshall's niece. I didn't know of my aunt's illness until just now."

She was interrupted by a glad cry from her aunt. "Linn, Linn!" Linn bent to kiss her aunt and was encircled by two frail arms for a brief fervent embrace. Then Linn felt her aunt push her away slightly and Linn was looking into a pair of faded green eyes.

Kate Marshall laughed softly. "It is good to see you, Linn." Linn saw her straighten herself and then she spoke with a kind of pitiful dignity. "I'm afraid you have caught us at a rather bad time. I'm so sorry that I am sick like this and the house is a mess."

Linn realized suddenly that her aunt was painfully embarrassed and at a loss as to what to do with her unannounced guest, even if she was a relative. She spoke quickly to put her at ease.

"Aunt Kate, I couldn't help but overhear and I want to help." She turned to the doctor. "Doctor, I have worked closely with a doctor in a small town in Idaho for the past three years. I'm a pretty good nurse and good at taking orders. Would it be possible to take care of my aunt here? She would be so much happier, having her daughter with her. I promise that I will see that she has everything she needs and follows your orders to a 'T,' " she finished in a rush. She saw him about to refuse, but after considering for a full moment, looking from patient to Linn and back again, he finally assented.

"I'm not sure that this is wise," he said, "but we will try it for a day or two. But if she is worse by then, it is to the hospital or I won't take the consequences!" With these parting words, he proceeded to outline a program for care of the patient and wrote out prescriptions for medicines.

Before he left, he drew Linn aside so her aunt could not hear and questioned her. "Young lady, do you have sufficient funds to take care of your aunt for several weeks? Your aunt is in a state of complete exhaustion. I doubt very seriously if she has any money. She is so proud that she would feel it an affront if I asked her. But if you need it I can probably get some help for them from the state Welfare Office. Medicines and proper food will be expensive."

Linn thanked him for his offer but told him she felt she

could swing the financial part for the present and when her aunt was better she was sure she could secure a position nearby to take care of expenses.

After seeing the doctor out, Linn went back to her aunt. She was shocked again to see how wasted and thin her aunt was. Her heart gave a lurch of fear. Had she taken on too much? Could she nurse this pitiful creature back to health again? Well, she would begin at once and give it a good try.

Linn sat down beside her aunt who lay with her eyes closed, as if she had not the strength to keep them open. The weary eyes opened and a slow smile spread over her face.

"Linn, I suppose I should be ashamed to let you take us on as an obligation like this, but I have been praying so hard for a miracle so I wouldn't have to leave Penny. I guess I had a silly fear that it would be like my sister—They put her in a hospital and put you temporarily in a home. She never lived to come out." Her voice trailed off weakly.

"Aunt Kate, I think you had better rest now. You—"

Her aunt raised a frail hand in protest. "I'm okay. Just a little tired. Now, Linn, I have a check due at the sewing factory. Penny can tell you the address. I want you to go and get that. That will take care of us for a bit. You aren't to shoulder the financial part of taking care of us. The work will be enough, and too much."

Linn laughed lightly to hide the catch in her throat. "I'll pick up the check. But don't you worry about a thing. I also am far from being broke and if I spend more than you think I should, you can pay me back when you're well and strong again. Okay?" She had no intention of letting her aunt pay her back but they could settle that when her aunt was well again. It apparently set her aunt's mind at ease, because she patted Linn's hand weakly.

"Now," Linn said, rising briskly, "I want you to go to sleep and let your new nurse get on with her job. You are not to worry about a thing. That is doctor's orders as part of the get-well treatment. Agreed?"

The patient smiled and softly said, "Agreed," and was almost instantly asleep.

Linn left Penny to watch her mother while she hurried to the drugstore four blocks away and left the prescriptions; then dashed next door to the grocer to pick up a few quick items to fix a lunch for the three of them. Oranges, canned soup, milk, and crackers would get them by until she saw what was in the cupboard and refrigerator. She suspected they would be comparative to Mother Hubbard's cupboard but to spare embarrassment to her newly-found cousin she hadn't asked or looked. Perhaps she could send Penny out on some pretense, while she looked over the larder.

Penny had told her the address of the sewing factory. Discovering by inquiry that the factory was nearby, Linn left the groceries at the store and went there. Obtaining the check was a small matter of only signing for it. Linn was shocked at the small amount of the check. It was no wonder that both cousin and aunt were so thin. It would be impossible to buy proper food and pay rent on that amount. And it was a check for two weeks' work!

When Linn arrived back at the store, she inquired if the store would cash the check if she sent Penny back with it and they quickly assented, as Mrs. Marshall was a regular customer. Linn stopped by the drugstore and picked up the filled prescriptions and hurried home.

The patient was sleeping the sleep of exhaustion. Linn put the milk in the refrigerator. The refrigerator was even more empty than Linn had imagined. There were only three items in it—a half used can of condensed milk, an almost empty bottle of ketchup and one egg in an open carton.

Linn quickly heated soup for lunch. She decided to let the mother sleep a bit longer before she woke her for lunch. Food was important but from the way she was sleeping, the rest was equally so. So she and Penny lunched on chicken noodle soup, crackers, milk and oranges. Penny ate shyly but hungrily. Afterward Linn woke her aunt. She ate a small amount but seemed too weary to care. She went quickly back to sleep after signing her check.

When lunch was over, Linn sent Penny to the store to cash the check. As soon as Penny was out of sight, Linn checked the cupboard for food. As Linn looked, a cold knot formed in her stomach. She wondered if her newly-found relatives had slowly been starving to death. If the cupboards were any evidence, this was certainly the case. Two cans of vegetables, a little flour, a handful of oatmeal, and one potato was the sum total of eatables. Linn sat at the table and made out a list of groceries. One thing she was sure of, no one could grow well and strong again without good food, and plenty of it.

When Penny returned, Linn roused her patient and gave her medicine and a glass of orange juice. Mrs. Marshall dropped off to sleep again immediately. Linn then freshened up, and leaving Penny to watch her mother, she walked a couple of blocks and caught a bus to a large supermarket that Penny had given her directions to. Even with return cab fare, she knew she would save a great deal on her large order of groceries. Economy must be practiced if she was to make her money stretch as far as it most likely would need to.

Linn arrived back home and, with Penny's help, had the groceries all stowed away before the patient woke up. Penny's eyes had been round with wonder at the very large order of groceries that had arrived with Linn. But she hadn't said a word—only made herself very helpful in putting them away. While Penny finished the last of the groceries, Linn seared a beef roast and put it in a slow oven to bake for supper. She wanted to get a good square meal under those thin little ribs of her shy small cousin.

The first night Linn had two patients for a while. Penny ate a hearty meal of the roast beef dinner and apparently her weakened stomach could not take that much rich food. So about bedtime she lost her whole supper. Linn was careful the next few days to see that she ate well but not so much.

Whenever her aunt awoke for the next several days, Linn tried to get something down her: fruit juice; warm broth; milk with fresh, raw egg, sugar and flavoring beat in. Kate also took a little solid food but only a few bites at a time as she seemed too exhausted to eat.

When the doctor returned the next day, he seemed pleased but warned Linn not to expect miracles. Mrs. Marshall had never been a strong woman, he said, and she had gone on nerve alone for it was anybody's guess how long. So it would take time and much rest and proper nourishment to build back her body.

Linn's days were filled with caring for her aunt and small cousin. The house was so small that at least it required little work. Penny was as much help as Linn would let her be.

Linn was pleased to see Penny's cheeks begin to fill out and color and vitality return, but she was alarmed because sometimes she didn't seem like a child at all. She seldom went out of doors but seemed to want to hover about her mother, worrying and fretting about her health.

Penny did like to read so Linn encouraged her to get books from the library which was within walking distance. At least she got fresh air, coming and going.

Most of the time Linn's days were happy, as she was so busy. But sometimes her nights were bad, because that was when she had time to think and remember. For now Linn remembered all of her past. Since those cruel last few moments with Clay and the storm of tears afterward, the barrier had been melted and she could recall even her early days of happiness with Clay—the bitter quarrels and the beautiful reconciliations. Sometimes, now, she tried to blot out the past because with the memories, bitter or sweet, longings rose in her heart that nothing could pacify. She realized that the life with Clay was a closed chapter that could never be reclaimed. Bitter tears, unbidden and unwelcome, wet her pillow many nights as she strove to forget now instead of remember.

Even with the vivid memories of Clay's harsh, acrimonious words ringing in her memory, Linn's love for Clay was not quenched. She tried to rationalize that Clay had been pushed almost beyond endurance—thus the harshness. If Clay only knew the truth he would not have acted as he did. He would still love her. Her heart refused to listen to reason.

So, night after night, Linn lay on her small rollaway bed and memories, some sweet and tender, others bitter and frightening (because many of these were brought about by manipulations of either Bonnie or Mrs. Randolph, Linn was certain now), flooded her mind. The only relief that Linn found from her loneliness and longing for her husband was in prayer. She would cry, silently so as not to disturb her aunt, until it seemed there were no more tears in her body. Then she would cry out to God who had been her Friend and Comforter for the past three years. He did not take away the longing but with His precious presence wrapping her in folds of love and understanding, she could bear the unbearable. She was comforted.

26

When Clay returned to the hospital, he found his mother resting well. She seemed to have shed her guilt feelings with her confession, and had slept all the time he was away, except for a brief time when the special nurse had awakened her for lunch.

After directing the special nurse to call him if his mother needed him and cautioning her to allow her no visitors, he left with a message that he would be back in a few hours.

Arriving back home, Clay questioned George and Mrs. Gray thoroughly but they had no idea where Linn had gone. George had presumed, as had Clay, that she would go the the doctor's house.

Clay went to Linn's room. Everything was in perfect order, and apparently Linn had taken nothing with her except the few things she had brought with her. All her former clothing still hung in the closet.

Checking the things on the dresser top, Clay saw, with a sharp pang in his heart, that Linn had left something else. Spread out was a small, rather soiled handkerchief with the letters *L.R.* in the corner. In the center lay Linn's wedding band, its jewels sparkling in the dappled sunlight from the window. Picking up the ring, Clay lived again the scene when he had last seen Linn. The shock of seeing the rings tumble from her pocket and the horror as he remembered his cruel words and Linn's pleading—and tears. Linn, who never cried, had pled with tears running down her face. And he, fool that he was, had driven her away, perhaps for good.

Would she ever forgive him if he did find her? She had regained her memory, of that he was certain, from some of her last words. She would remember now the humiliation and torment that she had endured at the hands of himself and his mother and Bonnie.

He ground his teeth in helpless fury and frustration. How could he have been such an utter fool, such an utter, complete FOOL! He felt like banging his head against the wall and tearing things to pieces!

He sat down upon Linn's bed and stretched out. He was very tired, body and spirit, but his relentless mind seemed bent on stern penance. He could not rest. He was as tense as a coiled spring and plans were formulated and discarded as quickly.

Finally he rose wearily, went downstairs and tried to eat the lunch Mrs. Gray had prepared. But after a few bites, his stomach rebelled at the sight of food, and he went to his study.

If only he could think of some feasible action to pursue, but there seemed to be nothing—nothing. There was no end to begin to unravel as to the whereabouts of Linn. She had just dropped out of sight.

"That's what you wanted, Clay Randolph. You told her to be gone when you returned and that you never wanted to see her again. You may get what you thought you wanted." It helped to read himself off, though it probably showed his state of mind.

He was brought from his brooding by a knock at the door. It was Mrs. Gray

"Mr. Randolph, have you checked to see if the orphanage might have the address of a relative that Miss Linn might have gone to see?"

Clay's haggard face lit up. He exclaimed, "Of course, why didn't I think of that!" And he sprang to the telephone, obtained the number quickly and was soon speaking with Miss Forrest, the superintendent of the home.

Clay tried to be calm as he spoke but his heart was pounding with excitement.

"Miss Forrest, this is Clay Randolph, Linn Randolph's husband. Could you tell me if you have the addresses of any relatives of Linn's?"

There was a lengthy pause at the other end of the line. Clay wondered if she was still on the line.

"Miss Forrest, are you still there?"

"Yes, I'm still here," The answer was curt. "Why, may I ask, do you want your wife's relative's address? Why don't you ask your wife for the address you want?"

Clay was taken aback. He hadn't meant to divulge his family problems and still didn't plan to. How much could he tell and get the desired results?

"My wife is away at the present and it is imperative that I obtain the address of her living relatives, now."

There was another pause as if the woman were debating what to do. Then she spoke crisply and decisively.

"I am sorry, Mr. Randolph, but I can't give out private information about our former inmates."

"But, I must have that information!" Clay cried urgently.

"Why is this so important to you?" came back the answer from that exasperating woman.

"I have every right to any information about Linn

Randolph. After all, she is my wife!"

There was that hesitancy again and then Miss Forrest spoke again firmly, "Mr. Randolph, I don't know what is going on in your family and it isn't any business of mine, except where it concerns one of our children. About three years ago, I gave some information to a woman, probably your mother, that I have since felt may have been used to discredit Linn. She is a fine girl and I don't want to make this mistake again. Any information you want about Linn or her family you must get from her, if she wants to give it to you. I am sorry I can't be of help to you. Goodbye." And before Clay could utter a word of protest, she hung up.

He rang back immediately but although she was polite, she was adamant and he didn't get the information he needed from her.

After hanging up the phone, he started pacing. It seemed that he couldn't be still. That woman had some information about at least one relative, Clay was sure, or she wouldn't have refused to give him information. So, Linn did have a living relative, and quite possibly in the area of the orphanage. But how could he obtain an address?

27

The first few days after Linn's arrival, Kate did very little but sleep and eat. She seemed to have given the problems over into Linn's hands, after her first embarrassment, and was sleeping the sleep of complete exhaustion. In fact, that is how the doctor explained her illness on one of his visits.

"This woman," he said, "has been going for a long while on spirit and spunk alone. Her body and mind have been worn to the breaking point but she could not let down until there was someone that she felt she could trust who could, and would, take over. When you arrived on the scene—in the nick of time, I would say—she relinquished her hold on the responsibility and her body finally conquered. Let her sleep all she will. Feed her something nourishing every time she awakens and don't let her know there is a care in the world that you can't take care of.

"The medicines I prescribed will be beneficial but her great need is the rest and nourishing food she is getting. If you can't swing the load financially, as I said before, I can get you some help. Our greatest problem right now is getting your aunt back on her feet. You are a God-send to her right now I guess you know that, young lady."

"I'm glad," said Linn, "and as for the financial help, I believe I can swing it alone. But I do appreciate the offer. I have a little saved."

But shortly Linn realized with a shock that she must be very careful with her savings, for after one week of caring for the needs of her aunt, her cousin, and herself, that little fund had dwindled dangerously. She would have to send for more money soon and her savings were not large. As soon as she could be spared, Linn would go back to work but that was out of the question until her aunt was much better, and her progress was slow. In the meantime, there was medicine, good nourishing food, rent, and utilities that must be paid for. So Linn carefully budgeted her money and shopped as frugally as possible and still provide nutritious meals.

The good wholesome meals were paying off in the appearance of Linn's little cousin. Perhaps the lessening of carrying a burden too large for her fragile shoulders was a help also.

Clay was at the end of his rope. Linn had been gone for four weeks now and Clay was as far from knowing where she was as he had been in the beginning. He had called the orphanage repeatedly, hoping that Miss Forrest would finally give in and give him the address of Linn's relative, but she stood as resolute in her first decision as the Rock of Gibraltar. Of course, Clay did not know that she was at this relative's home, but that was the only hint that he had of where she might be. She could be in some far city, trying to forget that he and his mother ever existed, trying to rebuild her life from the ruins he and his had perpetrated, for all he really knew.

Dr. Glover and his wife had given him their time freely and gladly whenever he felt like calling or visiting. They also had called and followed up on every possibility, however dim, but they also knew no one else to call, no place else to look. But there was one diffrence in their approach. They expected that sometime, somewhere, God would work things out. They assured him, over and over, that God knew where she was and that God would watch over her. They also urged him to put his trust in God.

This he could not do. He wasn't even sure there was a God but if there was, he was convinced that God did not bother Himself with the problems of His poor earthly creations. No, Clay did not buy this "God is concerned about you" bit. He was an intellectual, and was constantly amazed that a man of Dr. Glover's obvious intelligence could believe so emphatically the simple story that Dr. Glover had tried so earnestly to "sell" Clay; that man was a fallen creation but that God so loved man that His only son came to earth, in the form of a man, and died in his stead so man could be reconciled to God. That the Glovers believed this explicitly, Clay was sure. Sometimes Clay found himself wishing—even yearning—to believe, because he needed peace of mind so desperately. But he could not.

Eric was still handling much of Clay's work load, but four weeks after Linn's disappearance Clay thought, as he arose one morning from a weary bed of little sleep and troubled dreams, that he had to get back into the business of living again. It wasn't fair to Eric to constantly push all the work of running the family business onto Eric's overworked schedule. He would try this morning to get some work done. He dressed quickly and visited his mother for a few minutes, who was much improved but still rested much. Though he didn't want it, he downed a few bites of breakfast and joined Eric in the office.

Eric looked up with delight to see his friend and employer appear for work. They worked for several hours in the old comfortable way, when suddenly Clay stood up and threw down the book he was working on with a vicious slam, and stalked quickly from the room. Moments later, Clay's car was spinning down the road spurting gravel and burning rubber.

Clay had no idea where he was going or what he was going to do. He just felt that he had to do something—anything—to relieve the pressure that the frustrations and guilt and disappointments of the past four weeks had built up in his mind and body. His body felt like a bomb, set to go off at any moment. His mind was so tormented and mixed up that he felt that it, too, would blow into a million bits if something didn't happen to relieve the awful pressure. It was a seething caldron of tumbling, tormenting thoughts, longings, and vivid, haunting images of Linn—Linn laughing, Linn crying, Linn—Linn—Linn.

Clay drove like one pursued by howling demons over winding, twisting roads until he was in a dense woods. He slammed the brakes on—the car's walls were pressing in on him—and practically fell out the door and began to run, run, run. He ran, the branches and brush whipping him in the face and tearing at his clothes, falling at times but arising to run on and on—until finally he fell to the ground in a state of complete exhaustion. His lungs were on fire and his breath was coming in great gasps.

He lay there, gasping for breath, smarting and bleeding from numerous scratches, and came to the slow realization that he wanted to die, longed to die, willed to die. He felt that total extinction was the only answer to his agony. For what was life without Linn? Nothing! Sobs rose up in his throat and he had no power to stop them. They overpowered him and shook him in spasms of grief. Images of Linn rose in his tormented mind again and he began to voice his thoughts.

"Linn, where are you, where are you?" Sobs tore him apart but he continued to give voice to his anguish. "The doctor said God knows where you are. God! God!"

His mind clutched at this straw—God! God? Did God really care where she was? Did God really care? Could He—would He—help Clay find her? His mind fastened on this new thought like a drowning man. "God—God, please, God, if You're up there—if You really care, please help me to find her, please. Please—"

And now a new thought loomed into his conscious- ness—big and ugly and frightening. Why should God do anything for Clay Randolph? Clay, who had never cared about God. Clay Randolph was a fallen, sinful creature, not fit for God to even look upon. He saw himself as God must see him and as he writhed under the penetrating eyes of God, he began pleading with God to forgive him, to change him, to make him fit for God to look upon. Hadn't Dr. Glover said that God loved so much that He gave His Son to bring man back to God? Yes—yes that was what he had said!

"God—God—I need you—I need you—please, forgive me— "

The sun had been high when Clay fell to the ground on rough pine needles, but when finally the struggle ceased, it was very low. His sobs and wild cries had slowly subsided as a strange but altogether sweet and powerful presence brought peace—oh, such blessed peace! Clay Randolph, the intellectual, skeptical, wealthy businessman, had met God and found Him very real and very satisfying.

Now Clay felt like laughing and laugh he did—joyous, glorious laughter of one who has been through the torments of Hell but raised to live again. Forgiven! That's what he felt! Forgiven! and clean, and oh-so peaceful. He knew now how his mother could bear to face the scorn of her only son—to obtain this peace. This was what Linn had, what the Glovers had tried to tell him about!

At last Clay arose from the ground and walked to a small stream nearby and tried to make himself presentable enough to appear in public. His shirt was torn, his pants were stained and dirty, and he smarted from a dozen scratches. He washed his face and hands, brushed the leaves and twigs from his clothes and hair and went to find his car. It took him nearly an hour to find it so it was nearly dark before he was back on the road again.

He knew his mother and Eric would be worried about him but he decided to go immediately to tell the Glovers about his new-found faith.

It was a very startled doctor's wife who opened the door to a tattered, still besmudged, but radiant Clay, a while later.

"You've found Linn!" She exclaimed when she saw his glowing face. That usually reserved dignified young man threw his arms around the startled lady and half shouted, "I've found God!"

The Glovers were overjoyed and would not be satisfied until he told them the whole story.

"And I know I'll find Linn, now. I just know it!"

The doctor was silent for a long moment. Then he laid his hand on Clay's shoulder. "Clay, what if you never found Linn. Would you still serve God?"

Clay looked stunned and burst out, "But God wouldn't let that happen! I know He wouldn't."

"Perhaps not," the doctor said softly, "but God's ways are not always our ways. Could you serve God if God never brought Linn back to you?"

Clay's face paled. He turned away and went to stand at the window, deep in thought for several moments. His friends waited. At last he turned back to them. His voice was low. The words came slowly, haltingly as if he were feeling his way along.

"You probably think that I just came to God to get His help in this situation. At first that was my motive. That and nothing more. But that was before I really met Him. What I received this afternoon was the forgiveness God promised through His Son. That was a transaction between God and me. It had nothing to do with Linn. I will serve God regardless of what happens. It would be hard to never see Linn again, but I now believe God will be with me and see me through whatever comes."

The doctor searched Clay's face. Satisfied with what he saw, he spoke again gravely. "I do not know what God has planned for you but be patient, and whatever comes will be for both your and Linn's good. And remember, we are here anytime you need us, to pray with you or however we can help."

Clay looked from one to the other and knew that they meant it.

28

Linn was preparing breakfast one morning, about six weeks after she had come to her aunt, when she heard a voice in the sickroom. Stepping instantly to the doorway, Linn inquired, "Did you say something, Aunt Kate?"

Kate turned her head slowly on the pillow. "I said, I'm not going to die, after all."

As Linn swiftly crossed the room to the bedside, she observed with delight that Kate's green eyes were bright and alert. For these many weeks she had laid in almost a stupor, even when awake, seemingly too tired and emotionally drained to care whether she lived or died. Indeed, she seemed almost unaware of what went on around her.

Linn stooped to kiss her aunt's gaunt cheek. "Of course, you're not going to die! That's something we don't allow around here, young lady."

Kate smiled up at her niece. "This is the first time in months that I wasn't sure that death was only a step away."

Linn sat down on the edge of the bed and, taking one of her aunt's thin, lined hands in her own warm ones, she spoke softly, "You were utterly exhausted. You have had a close call. But I never thought for a minute that God would give me a family and then allow you to be snatched from me."

"Yes, I have been on the edge of collapse for a long

while. I have gone through each day not knowing if I could struggle through." Kate's voice broke with emotion. "I fought so hard because I was afraid for Penny. I kept remembering my sister—your mother. They took her away to a hospital and she never left it alive. I knew how painful the adjustment was for you, living in an orphanage. Penny is a frail child and very dependent on me. My heart just broke at the thought of her being raised among strangers."

Kate's voice quavered, "And then you miraculously appeared, in answer to my desperate prayer. Whenever I woke up, there you were—strong, competent, and so gentle and sweet." Her eyes flooded wth tears. "How can I ever repay you or thank you enough for what you have done?"

Linn was deeply touched. "Aunt Katie, it has been a joy to feel needed. You and Penny are my family. That is ample pay!"

"Now," Linn spoke in her best nurse voice. "It is time my patient had a good breakfast. What will it be, steak and eggs?" she ended teasingly.

That afternoon Kate was able to sit up for a few minutes and her recovery, though not an overnight thing, moved forward steadily from that day.

Three weeks had passed since Clay's stupendous conversion. The rosy glow had gradually slipped away from his experience but in its place a strong healthy trust was growing. And trust he must, because he was no closer to finding Linn than he had been three weeks before.

He was still badgering the orphanage superintendent, Miss Forrest, and Glenn Trestle at the bank, but both were as adamant as before.

Clay had told his mother and also Eric, in a few words, of his conversion. He still could not feel completely comfortable in confiding his thoughts and feeling to his mother. He felt he had forgiven her but there was still a reserve he felt with her, perhaps even a distrust. He wasn't sure what it was. He needed someone to talk with when every avenue still continued to be blocked but he just could not discuss Linn with his mother. He hoped that someday he would feel a closeness with her again but now he did not and that was that.

He used to talk quite freely with Eric, who had long been his closest friend as well as employee. But he could not talk freely about Linn with him either. Clay was no longer the same person and his relationship with Eric seemed changed, someway.

The Glovers were willing to talk with him, and he did call them now and then but he knew they were busy people, the only doctor in their community, so Clay felt he could not abuse their kindness and friendship.

So Clay learned to pray, out of necessity. He began to practice discussing everything aloud with God. He told Him about his terrible longing for Linn, and, at times, his despair of ever finding her. And he never failed after a time of pouring out his thoughts, feelings, hopes, discouragements and fears, in receiving a refreshing and ever-increasing confidence that God was in control and that he, Clay Randolph, and Linn were under His watchful care.

And one day as Clay rose from his knees, where he had fallen a while before in a state of complete despair and discouragement, he felt a strange exultation. He stood by his window and looked out into the deepening twilight and felt the feeling grow into an assurance. He knew. How, he could not say, but he knew, beyond a shadow of a doubt, that he would see Linn again! When, how, or where, he did not know but see her he would! And this time, with God's help, he would try not to blow it!

A week passed and then two. He called Miss Forrest and Mrs. Trestle again with the same negative results. He talked with the Glovers again, and even questioned his mother and Eric and his two house servants and even old uncle Arthur again to see if they could remember any scrap of conversation or anything that might have been forgotten. This was negative, also. Clay should have been discouraged but when he was tempted to be, this same feeling of assurance came quietly into his consciousness. He marveled; and though he could not have explained it to anyone, or to himself, either, for that matter, he just knew that he would see Linn again. At times he felt impatience trying to push in but he would not allow it. His faith needed to be strong, and impatience, he was finding, was a hindrance to his peace of mind. Clay was learning what many people never learn, to simply trust God.

Miss Forrest was troubled. She had steadfastly refused to divulge to Linn's husband any information about Linn's only living relative, because she felt it somehow might be used against Linn. But when Clay had called the past three times, she had sensed that there was a subtle change in him, an indefinable "something" that made it increasingly hard to deny him the information he requested.

This morning Miss Forrest lay in bed. She had awakened early, as was her custom, but had rolled over to a more comfortable position, when she remembered it was her day off work, and had tried to go back to sleep. But an uneasy apprehension invaded her spirit and she finally sat up and tried to think what was causing it. Then she remembered. Ever since Mr. Randolph had called several days before, she had had this strange feeling that she couldn't shake. She went over the conversations she had had with Linn's husband and chided herself out loud.

"Now, Lucy, I want you to stop worrying about not giving that man Linn's aunt's address. If Linn wanted him to have it she would give it to him."

And then a new thought came to her. Perhaps Linn had left her husband and he was trying to find her. Wasn't that a good enough reason for her to give him an address where he might find her? No! She, Lucy Forrest, had no right to meddle in the affairs of her former charge.

Lucy got out of bed, fixed herself some coffee, fed her cat, and put him out. She straightened her small apartment, then eagerly took down the book she had been looking forward to reading all week. She stretched out on her comfortable couch, adjusted the shade on her reading lamp and began to read. She had read but a few lines when the uneasy restlessness crept back in her being. Angrily, she tried to will it away, continuing to read. She started to turn the page and realized she couldn't remember a thing that she had read.

Lucy swung herself to a sitting position and demanded: "Lucy, in the name of good sense, what is the matter with you!"

She heard the faint scratch of her cat at the door and rose to let him back in, then went to sit in her rocker by the window. She could see the children playing in the playground. Suddenly she felt that she needed to get away from the orphanage. Yes, that was what she needed. Surely that was it! That was why things like those calls of Clay Randolph were getting to her. She would get away for a couple of days.

But where should she go? There was no place she really wanted to go. Her best friend worked here at the orphanage too, and had different days off, so she would have to go alone. Her brief feeling of elation faded. She went to the kitchen and made herself another cup of coffee, carried it to a little table near the rocker and sat down again, rocking aimlessly for a few minutes, sipping her coffee. The restlessness and unease crept back into her being as softly as her cat had crept into her lap without her being aware of him. She stroked his glistening fur absently and the cat arched his back and purred in ecstasy. Unheeding, Lucy rocked thoughtfully.

For the hundredth time in the past few days, her thoughts turned to Linn and Clay Randolph. "Maybe I should just ask Mr. Randolph, pointblank what he wants that address for," she murmured. "No," she contradicted herself. "That was a falsehood his mother gave that other time for information, I'm sure. How could I be sure he would be truthful? If only there was a way to check the matter out," she mused aloud. "If I could only talk to the aunt or Linn and find out what is going on."

Suddenly she jumped to her feet dumping the indignant cat from her lap. "Of course! Why didn't I think of that before! I need a change and that's a good excuse for getting away. I'll go to Allenville and go to see Linn's aunt. I'll do a bit of sleuthing on my own!" A spirit of high adventure beat in her bosom as she went to pack an overnight bag.

Kate lay on the worn couch in her tiny sparsely-furnished living room. She was still very weak, but much improved. For a week now she had been sitting up for longer and more frequent periods each day. And now she was hungry, ravenously so, much of the time. The nourishing food that Linn was constantly plying her with, had already begun to fill out her pinched face and slight form. She still slept a great deal, but when she awoke now she was alert and conscious of all that went on in her small world.

Linn had gone to the store for her weekly grocery supply. Kate was lying on the couch where Linn had placed her before she left. Penny was reading, curled up in the large worn old chair near the window. Kate had lain quietly for several moments, resting from the exertion of the brief walk from the bed to the couch.

Kate was thinking of Linn. Linn had said nothing at all to Kate of her life the past several years. Kate noticed she wore no wedding ring and yet she knew that Linn had married more than three years before. She had always been very concerned about her niece and had contacted the orphanage and case workers regularly for news of her welfare.

Linn had never answered any of her letters as she was angry with Kate for letting her be placed in a home. When Linn had married, Kate had only received a card telling her about it, after the wedding—and no return address. She had not been invited to the wedding. So it had been a great shock when Linn had appeared at just the opportune time and lovingly and expertly brought help to Kate and Penny.

At first Kate had been too ill to concern herself with why Linn had come to them, except as a miraculous answer to her cry to God. But as Kate's health improved, she begun to wonder, and remember the old rebellious, angry child of years past. Linn did not act at all like the old Linn.

The Linn that moved about her home so efficiently was very obviously at peace with God and herself. Not once had her temper flared or impatience showed, even in the most try-ing times. At times, a sadness showed in her eyes, and twice, Kate was sure there was a trace of tears when she first rose in the morning but she was as cheerful and kind as ever.

Had Linn's marriage floundered? Was that the cause of the sadness? Kate wished that Linn would confide in her but she was sure her niece would not until Kate was much stronger. That would be Linn's way. She would not burden Kate with her problems because she would not want her troubled.

Kate's heart swelled with love and gratitude as she meditated on the great service Linn was doing. Her heart shuddered to think what would have happened to them if Linn had not come. She would like so much to repay her when she was well and strong again. Or at least take the burden of supplying their financial needs away from Linn. She wondered how Linn was managing to buy the nutritious food that she prepared so deliciously and abundantly. And the rent and utilities. A small kernel of worry began to form in Kate's mind. Could she be going in debt for them? Then she remembered Linn's reassuring laugh when she had asked her a few days before about how she was managing to meet the bills.

"Don't you worry your pretty head about bills, dear Auntie," she had said, "I have a little saved and when we need more, I'll go out and get a job. You'll be able to be the housekeeper by then." Linn was a Christian, and Christians don't lie, so what had she, Kate, to worry about? Perhaps it was wrong to let Linn pay for everything and have the load of everything, but Kate knew that Linn's coming was an answer to prayer. Therefore she felt she should accept what God had sent, until she could manage to take over the load of her own and Penny's care again.

This simple reasoning eased her mind and the kernal of worry dissolved. Kate laid back and thanked God over and over, silently. How good God was to her, not only in sending help just when she needed it most, but in giving her back the love and affection of her niece that she had loved from afar so long.

A spasm of pain crossed her face as she remembered why she could not take Linn when Linn's mother had died. Kate's husband had been alive then.

Her husband, Frank, had never been an easy man to get along with. He had a violent temper, drank heavily, and spent much of his money for drink. He was an unskilled laborer and out of work periodically so money was scarce at best. So when Kate had approached him about taking her sister's orphaned daughter in, he had raved and stormed and refused vehemently, finally stalking out to get drunk. Kate had tiny, newborn Penny to care for and was not strong herself, so she knew it was impossible to take Linn in and risk having what little support she had removed. She was not able to support a family and care for a new baby.

So she had to bear the pain of seeing her only sister's child put in a home because she was helpless to prevent it. Linn had not understood. This was why Kate was still amazed and marveled at this "new" Linn. She bore no malice, and she lovingly and gladly had taken over the care of an aunt that as far as she knew had deserted Linn in her hour of need and let her be placed in a "Home" among strangers. Well, it all just showed that there was no end to the miracles God could perform!

Linn's father, Lewis Bell, had still been living when Linn's mother had died in a tuberculosis sanitarium, but he had left his wife and daughter just before his wife had been placed in the sanitarium. Indeed, that is probably what hastened Linn's mother's death. Linn's father had also been a drinking man and finally "drink" had become his only desire, so he had left his wife and daughter and was dead within a year, killed in a drunken brawl. But at least Linnie had been spared the news of his death because she had died a short while before. She had still loved her alcoholic husband and always asked, when Kate visited her, if there was any news of Lewis.

Kate was suddenly shaken from her commiserations by a sharp knock on the door. Penny looked up from her book.

"I'll go see who it is, Mother," she said as she hopped up from her chair.

"Don't let anyone in until I say it's OK," cautioned her mother.

Kate couldn't see the caller but when the person spoke, she knew instantly that the voice was familiar, though she couldn't place it at first.

"Is your mother in?" inquired a woman's crisp voice.

Penny turned to her mother questioningly. Kate answered her look with a soft, "Ask for her name."

But the visitor's sharp ears had heard and answered before Penny could ask.

"Tell her that Miss Forrest from the Children's Home wishes to speak with her."

Kate motioned for Penny to ask her in. Penny unlatched the screen door and stood back to allow Miss Forrest to enter. Penny politely but shyly drew up a small rocker near her mother for the visitor and withdrew to her own old worn chair.

The two women exchanged greetings. Kate apologized for lying down. The amenities over, Miss Forrest was ready to get down to the reason for her visit.

"I have really come to see Linn. Is she here?" inquired Miss Forrest.

Kate hesitated, then asked a question of her own. "Is there some kind of trouble?"

"Well, I'm not sure," responded Miss Forrest truthfully. "Her husband has been trying to get me to give him your address for several weeks. I didn't feel it was my business to give out information about my former charges. I felt Linn would give any information she wished him to have. And then it occured to me yesterday that he might be trying to reach Linn through you. But I didn't want to give him any information until I had talked to you or Linn."

"Linn is here with me, Miss Forrest," Kate said. "She has been caring for Penny and me. I have been very sick. Linn is at the grocery store but she should be home soon. Could Penny make you a cup of coffee?"

"I would love some if you would have some with me."

"I'll have my morning juice. Linn is a hard nurse. She plies me with something to eat or drink every time I wake up but she won't let me have any coffee, except at breakfast." Kate laughed.

When Linn walked in a few minutes later, she was surprised to find Kate and Miss Forrest sipping their drinks and chatting.

Miss Forrest told her errand. Linn's heart contracted painfully when she heard that Clay had been trying for several weeks to secure Kate's address from Miss Forrest. She was silent for several long seconds as she fought to still the pain in her heart. Then she said bluntly, "Clay and I separated several weeks ago. It is not my desire, but I am sure Clay is trying to reach me to begin divorce proceedings." She paused, drew in a sharp breath and laughed a little, self-consciously. "I left no address and I suppose I haven't really wanted him to find me. I wanted to put off the whole distasteful thing."

"Is there no hope that things can be worked out, Linn?" her aunt asked hopefully.

"I wish there was," Linn said, "but I'm afraid there is no hope for that. It is a long story and I don't feel like going into it."

"Shall I just stall your young man and give you more time to try to work things out?" asked Miss Forrest. "Sometimes it pays to just wait and—"

Linn interrupted, "I'm afraid that all the time in the world wouldn't heal this breach. It had been three years and then we almost got back together and something happened to make it worse than ever. No, it is over for good."

Everyone was silent for a moment, then Linn spoke brightly, or tried to. "Now you two don't worry about me. I'm happy right here, riding herd on Aunt Kate. When she is well, I'll get a job and be busy and I'll be fine. After all, I still have a family, and I'll stay right here if Penny and Aunt Kate will have me."

A small form sprang from the big chair and flung her arms around Linn's neck crying, "Of course we want you. Please don't leave us, Linn! We couldn't bear it if you went away. Please stay, Linn, please—" The torrent of words had turned into tears and the small arms were threatening to choke Linn.

Linn drew away the clinging arms and mingled a few tears with Penny's as she assured her that she had no intention of going anywhere.

When she had calmed her small cousin, still holding her on her lap, Linn spoke to Miss Forrest, "Would you mind calling Clay for me? Good! I would rather not talk to him. We parted under rather traumatic conditions. Tell him I will meet with his lawyer at any time but not here. My aunt is sick so I don't want him coming here. There is a small cafe about a block from my aunt's house. I will meet with his lawyer there. I'll give you the name and address of the cafe and his lawyer can call there and leave me word when he wants to meet me. I'll make arrangements with the owner of the cafe. She is a very nice person and I'm sure that will be OK. But under no circumstances must he come here. I will refuse to see him if he does. Would you tell him that, Miss Forrest? Call him collect. He won't mind, I'm sure, as he will want to get this thing expedited."

Miss Forrest reluctantly agreed and suggested going to the nearest phone and calling immediately. Linn remembered seeing a pay phone in that little cafe. So Miss Forrest left, promising to return to tell the results of her call.

29

When the call came, Clay was in the office talking over a business matter with Eric. Clay answered the phone. A slightly familiar voice of a woman was on the line asking to speak with Clay Randolph. Clay felt his pulse quicken for some reason as he identified himself.

"Mr. Randolph, this is Lucille Forrest from the Children's Home. You have been asking for the address of your wife's only living relatives. Do you still want that information?"

Clay replied tersely, "Very definitely."

The voice at the other end hesitated as if arranging her words, "Do you wish to contact your wife or did you just want the address you asked for?"

Clay felt his hand holding the phone begin to tremble with emotion. Was he about to find Linn after all these fruitless weeks? His heart beat hard in his own ears. "I really want to contact my wife."

The voice became business-like now as if sure of her ground. "Very well. I have seen Mrs. Randolph and she sent a message to you."

Clay felt every muscle of his body tense like a coiled spring and tried to relax. "Yes, please go on."

"She said she would meet with your lawyer whenever it was convenient for him but that it must be at a small cafe near her aunt's house where she is staying. Her aunt has been very ill and is still weak so Linn would not want anyone to visit her there."

"But I must see Linn myself. She will see me, won't she?"

When the voice did not answer immediately, Clay demanded again, "She will see me, won't she?"

Miss Forrest sounded uncertain, "Why, I really don't know. She didn't expect that you would come. She seemed certain you would send a lawyer."

Clay forgot that he had not told Miss Forrest, forgot that he didn't want to discuss his family problems with a stranger, indeed, forgot everything but that he wanted to see Linn and that this woman knew where she was. He blurted out in an anguished voice, "I don't need a lawyer! I just want to talk to Linn! I want my wife back."

Miss Forrest drew in her breath sharply and felt a warm glow start somewhere in the vicinity of her heart. "You mean you would like a reconciliation with Linn?"

"Yes, yes! That's exactly what I mean! Now, please give me her address so I can go to her."

Miss Forrest said, "Linn said explicitly that she would not see anyone at her aunt's house so I'll give you the name and address of the cafe. I hope that will be all right with her. You can call the cafe with information about when you will meet, or if you wish I can give her the message."

"I'll tell you now," said Clay. "Just give me a minute to figure how long it will take to reach there. Where is she?"

Miss Forrest gave him the address in Allenville. He considered briefly and then said, "Tell Linn the appointment will be at nine o'clock in the morning. And please do not tell her that I am coming or what I want. She might not see me. There have been some very unpleasant happenings and I couldn't really blame her if she wouldn't see me, but with God's help I hope to straighten out a few things."

Late that night Linn laid sleepless on her narrow bed. She had tried unsuccessfully to will herself to sleep for hours. This was one night she almost wished she did not have her memory back. As the memories poured through her mind, she had to confess reluctantly to herself that she had not fully accepted the fact that her life with Clay was over. She had thought she had accepted the fact, but now she realized why she had not let Clay know—or anyone, for that matter— where she was; she was putting off the inevitable termination of her marriage with Clay.

She loved Clay. In spite of his apparent abhorence for her, she loved him with all her heart, irrevocably, eternally, it seemed. That she could still love him after the way he had spoken to her in those last minutes was inconceivable and incomprehensible but that she did love him with all her being, she knew. It seemed her heart would break with longing for him. The pain and loneliness that she had felt was now a burning, agonizing pain, so intense that it was a physical pain. She was now face to face with the knowledge that tomorrow she would be seeing Clay's lawyer, to sever her ties to Clay forever.

When Miss Forrest had returned to the house briefly before returning home, to tell her that her appointment was the following morning, she had borne up courageously because she didn't want her aunt or Penny to worry about her. She had felt numb with shock that the appointment was so soon, but had tried to speak calmly and had succeeded quite well, she thought, though her innermost being was being torn to pieces. Even a few days to get used to the idea of a permanent separation would have helped.

After she had thanked Miss Forrest and Miss Forrest had gone on her way, Linn had put away groceries, prepared the evening meal, done the dishes with Penny's help and talked and listened to Penny's chatter, in a sort of daze. She had shut the door on the thoughts that tried to enter—indeed that clamored to get in—and did automatically the things that needed doing, thankful for them so she need not think of Clay.

But soon, too soon, her Aunt Kate and Penny were both in bed and though Linn looked around almost frantically for something to keep herself busy and her mind occupied, there was nothing except a little mending to do and that only kept her fingers busy. So Linn went to bed, hoping that sleep would come quickly.

But as soon as she stretched out, the floodgates were rudely smashed aside and the floods of memories poured in, bittersweet and haunting. Since regaining her memory she had never let her mind dwell much on the whirlwind courtship when Clay, handsome and vitally alive, had swept her off her feet, or the early days of her marriage to Clay when she had gone from day to day blissfully loving Clay with an intense, ecstatic love and had been loved in return just as ardently. Nothing had marred those days, not even the knowledge that Clay's mother did not approve the marriage. She had felt that love like theirs could sweep aside all obstacles and create miracles. She would make Mrs. Randolph love her. And she might have succeeded had Bonnie not returned from back east to attend her mother's funeral.

Through her mind whirled the memories of violent quarrels with Clay; the hopelessness and despair when she knew that Bonnie and Mrs. Randolph were conspiring to destroy her marriage; the horror of being accused of being a kleptomaniac and the greater horror as she saw Clay begin to draw away from her and align himself with his mother and Bonnie. She vividly recalled Mrs. Randolph's heart attack; the agonizing break with Clay; herself hiding the rings, and being backed to the end of the dock by that strange person demanding the ring.

Now she tried hard to recall just how the person had looked. Perhaps there was a need to remember. Had that person pushed her off the dock and she had fallen into the boat, or had he—or she—struck her on the head and placed her in the boat and sent it out into the current to what, without God's intervention, would have been certain death? Who was the person and why did he—or she—want the ring?

She sorted out her remembrances. The person was not tall so it could not have been Clay. She could not remember clearly but her impression was that the figure was of average height though she could not be sure, because of the hat.

Who would have wanted the ring? Clay, of course, but he was ruled out because of height and also because that would not be like him. He would have come with no deceit and confronted her.

Bonnie would have wanted it because that was her first request when Linn had come back after her three year's absence. Linn thought hard. Could it have been Bonnie? She might have done something like that but Linn was almost certain that her tiny figure would not have appeared as large as she remembered the strange person.

Mrs. Randolph would have wanted the ring but she probably would not have chanced leaving her sick bed when things were going her way, especially. And besides, the figure had given the impression of being thinner than Mrs. Randolph's plump figure.

It could have been the housekeeper, of course, but it was hard to imagine stern-faced, practical Mrs Gray doing something mysterious like that had been. But perhaps it could have been her. She was very loyal to Mrs. Randolph and Clay.

There were only three other persons at the house at the time. George, who could not be a suspect because he was Linn's friend. Eric was there but again he was tall, even taller than Clay. There was only one other person in the house. And Linn smiled to consider him. Poor, addle-brained, pathetic Uncle Arthur, who moved in an alcoholic haze and was seldom aware, it seemed, of the world around him.

It was hard to know from her vague impressions, and after a three-year time lapse, who the person had been. It was also difficult to decide if her winding up in the boat and being carried down the river to an almost certain death had been an accident or intentional. Whether accident or intentional, the person had certainly not told Clay. Linn knew he would have told her when she was on good terms with him before the supposed thefts began again.

Well, perhaps she would never know. Maybe it was better for her not to know. Tomorrow she was closing that chapter of her life. Her heart lurched in pain at the thought. But she must face the inevitable. Clay was going out of her life. She would probably never see him again. She tried to speak sternly to herself: Linn, face up to this thing like a

Christian. God will help you. Clay is going out of your life forever. He is divorcing you! That does not have to end life for you. God will help you rebuild your life so it is meaningful again.

But she got no further. All the sternness and the practical words meant nothing to her heart. All the longing and hurt of her heart swelled up within her and she felt she wanted to die if she had to give up her husband. Her heart seemed to break into a thousand pieces; her body convulsed with sobs. She tried to stop the flow of tears and suppress the sobs that tore at her, but they refused to be stopped. She buried her face in her pillow to muffle the cries that came through her unwilling lips. Her body shook with sobs. I can't wake Aunt Kate, she tried to tell herself, but the grief would not be stilled. Suddenly she felt a hand on her head and she lifted her tear-drenched face to see Aunt Kate, wrapped in an old quilted bathrobe, kneeling beside her bed.

Linn, very concerned to see her aunt out of bed, began to beg her to go back to bed and tried to apologize, all in the same breath, for waking her.

Aunt Kate put a cool thin hand on Linn's hot forehead and pushed back her hair from her wet face before she said softly, "Linn, honey, I'm perfectly all right. Now you just let those tears come. That's what God made them for, to wash away our grief. Just lay your head on Aunt Kate's shoulder and have that good cry. It will do you good."

The tenderness in her voice and the concern on her face were too much for Linn and she burst into tears again Aunt Kate's gentle arms went about her and gathered her close. The torrent of tears did not last long, because in her aunt's gentle, tender embrace, Linn felt the emptiness and loneliness of the past few hours slip magically away. The sorrow of losing Clay was still with her but the pain was now bearable.

After a while she lifted her face and spoke shakily, "My, I'm sure a cry-baby. I haven't been able to sleep, thinking about tomorrow, and the divorce—and all." Her voice broke on the word "divorce" but she regained her composure and went on, "I thought I had reconciled myself to the thought that our separation was for good but I hadn't, I guess. But I'm all right, now, and you had better get back to bed."

Aunt Kate patted her hand gently, "I'm quite comfortable here on this rug so don't worry about me. Linn, I want you to remember that we are your family and want to help you through this time of adjustment. If you feel it would help to talk about it, that is what I am for. Sometimes it helps to spill it out, sort of a release. Do you want to share it with me, Linn? I don't wish to impinge on your privacy but if you want to talk about it, my ear is available."

Linn laughed a shaky laugh. "You sound so much like Mrs. Glover that it makes me a little homesick." At Kate's quizzical look, Linn hastened to explain. "I have been with a doctor and his wife for three years—the Glovers. If you really want to listen I will tell you about it." When Kate assured her she did, Linn first tucked her into the old chair near the bed, with a quilt wrapped around her. Then she told her briefly about herself and Clay, how she happened to be with the Glovers and how she came to be back in the Randolph house again. She didn't hide any part of it but told it as briefly and impassionately as she could. Though it hurt her deeply to talk about it, at the same time she felt a sort of "release," even as her aunt had said.

When she finished, her aunt sat for a moment deep in thought, sorting out the story in her mind. Then she reached over and laid her soft hand on Linn's hands clasped tightly together about her knees. "Linn, this has been a very heart breaking experience for you but through it all you found God. That makes it the most precious experience of your life. You still have a rocky time ahead but God will see you through. And Penny and I are here, too, to help in any small way we can.

"And, Linn," she went on, "you will never know what your coming to us when you did has meant to Penny and me. I was at the complete end of my strength. I prayed that

somehow God would spare Penny what you went through—
the foster homes, and orphanage. When you came in answer
to that prayer, it was like an angel straight from Heaven." Her
voice shook and tears filled her eyes. "God had never been
so real to me before. He answered my desperate prayer as I
was literally going down for the last time. I do thank God and
I thank you!"

Linn hugged her aunt. "And I needed a place to go to
lick my wounds Aunt Kate. Your house and a responsibility
were just what the doctor ordered, or maybe I should say
more correctly, what a loving, caring God, ordered. And to
have a family during this time is such a comfort." Settling
back on the bed, she pulled her legs up and wrapped her
arms around them. "You are what I imagine my mother
would have been like, had she lived, Aunt Kate."

Kate sat very still for a moment as she studied Linn for a
speculative, long moment. Then Kate seemed to make a
decision, and she leaned toward Linn. "Linn, I don't know
whether this is the time to tell you this but I think perhaps it
should have been told long ago." She hesitated and Linn
sensed that she was about to be told something momentous.

Kate sat back and closed her eyes. She seemed to be
lost in her thoughts and didn't speak again for some time.
Linn watched her and when she didn't go on, she began to
be apprehensive. Was her aunt over-exerting herself? Had
she become exhausted? She was about to ask her if she
wouldn't like to go back to bed, when Kate spoke.

"I don't know quite how to tell you this, Linn. So let me
just tell you what happened. "When Linnie, your mother,
became sick and was put in the tuberculosis hospital, she
was pregnant." Linn gasped, then restrained herself. "She
knew when she was admitted to the hospital that she would
not live, and she begged me to take the baby when she died.
Your father, as you probably remember, had left you both a
couple of months before. She knew that he would not take
responsibility for a new baby. In fact, she felt that may have
been why he left. He knew the baby was on the way.

"At the time, I was working. My husband by this time was a confirmed alcoholic and I had to work most of the time to keep food on the table. I told Frank that I planned to take Linnie's baby when it was born. He was very angry because I would have to quit work. And he never liked responsibility. But he grudgingly accepted my decision.

"I know, Linn, that you never understood why I could not take you when your mother was placed in the hospital. You were not told about the baby because your mother knew you would worry yourself sick about her had you known. So you were placed in a temporary foster home and I continued to work, trying to save enough to tide myself and a tiny baby over until it was old enough to be left in a nursery. Frank had gotten so bad with drink that many weeks he was scarcely sober enough to work even when he could get work. And most of his money went for alcohol.

"When the baby came, the doctor pronounced her a healthy baby, surprisingly, though very small and delicate. I took her home after a week, and of course had to quit work to care for her. Weakened by giving birth, Linnie only lived a week longer.

"I begged Frank to let me bring you home to care for, too. He didn't want the baby but he flatly refused to let you come. If there had been any way that I could have managed, I would have taken you anyway. But now I had to depend on Frank for our income, so I had to honor his wishes. Strangely, he did better than he had done in a long time and seemed to even care for little Penny for a time. For about two years I didn't work and just cared for Penny. She was a frail child though she was healthy."

She continued.

"But when Penny was about two, Frank got with some of his old friends and began to spend most of his time drinking again. One day he just left and never returned. I heard later that he had died from cirrhosis of the liver, the victim of alcohol. When Frank left, I went back to work, taking Penny with me when I could, and leaving her with friends or neighbors or a nursery when I had to. I haven't done too well for Penny but I have loved her and done the best I could. And I have thanked God nearly every day of my life for her. She has been my only real joy, except for the Lord."

Aunt Kate sat very still, waiting for Linn to speak. Linn finally spoke in a choked voice. "Then Penny is my very own sister?" When Kate nodded, she went on in a dazed, incredulous voice. "I have a sister! I should have known. She looks just like me! I loved her from the first but this is too marvelous to be true. I have a sister!"

Kate said softly, "I was afraid you would be angry because you weren't told. I have a confession to make. I was a little afraid you would try to take her from me after you grew up so I was afraid to tell you. The Linn that you used to be was a very mixed-up, angry person. God has changed you so much that you are not that person, anymore. Do you know that, Linn?"

"Yes," said Linn softly. "You were right not to tell the old Linn. If you had, you would not have Penny today. Sometimes, I wonder what Clay saw in her, I really can't blame him for not wanting me, for he hardly knows the new me. And the old Linn was a terror." she took a deep breath, "And now, Miss Kate, I'm your nurse, and a real old ogre. I'll have to answer to the doctor if you have a relapse, so back to bed with you, and make it snappy!"

30

When Clay turned from the telephone after Miss Forrest's call, his face was lit up like a neon light. He shouted, "I've found Linn!"

Eric sprang from his chair. But before he could comment, the door opened and Mrs. Randolph stood in the doorway. "Mrs. Gray said to tell you that supper is ready."

Then she noticed the expression on Clay's face. She looked at Eric and then back to Clay, and then said quietly, "You have found Linn."

Eric spoke excitedly, "Where is she, man? Don't hold us in suspense!"

"I'm to meet her in the morning in Allenville. Miss Forrest contacted her and set up a meeting. I'll fly over there in the morning."

Mrs. Randolph said softly, "I'm glad, Clay. Is Linn okay?"

"I'm sure she is," replied Clay. "Miss Forrest said that she has been caring for her aunt, who has been very sick. I'm to meet her at a nearby cafe, as she doesn't want the aunt to be bothered. She isn't expecting me. She thought I would be sending a lawyer, so I hope she will see me."

A spasm of pain crossed Mrs. Randolph's face. "I have prayed every day that God would undo the damage that I have done."

Clay crossed the room to face his mother. "Mother," he said sternly, "you musn't worry about this. What is done, is done, and nothing can change it. So we will put it all in God's hands and trust it there, Okay?"

Mrs. Randolph searched his face, then with a gentle smile assented that he was right. "At least one good thing has come of all this, we both have come to Christ," she said.

Eric stood by and listened to the turn of the conversation with an uneasy feeling. That Clay—or his mother, either, for that matter—should talk about God and Christ in such a familiar way was beyond him. He had never had any religious training. He had always believed in a higher power, but never as a personal "Someone" who concerned himself with the puny affairs of His creation. Clay had said little to him except to tell him that he had had a special experience up on the mountainside that day. Eric had laid it to the emotional state that Clay had been in that day. But whatever it had been, it had had a tremendous effect on Clay. Although Clay had still continued to try with all his might to find a trace of his wife, he had been able to resume his work and even seemed to be happy again.

And Eric had been amazed to see Clay going to a small church in Whitebird on Sundays, sometimes in company of his mother and when she was not able, alone. When he returned, Clay seemed to have gained something; he seemed serene and refreshed. Eric marveled. Although he declined to go with Clay, he had begun to wonder about this "religion" thing.

While he was intrigued with what it had apparently done for Clay and his mother, Eric drew back from becoming involved himself. He had always considered religious people as "off-beat' people who had to have a crutch to cope with life. And they were always trying to push it off on everyone. But neither Clay nor his mother had done this. Now that he puzzled over it, he remembered that Linn had also been so different that except for looking the same, she could hardly be recognizable as the same girl. He could still recall vividly the violent temper tantrums that she used to pull. Everyone for a city block could have heard her. But never once had she displayed the temper after her return. He was puzzled and almost longed to look into it for himself when pleasures palled at times and he wondered what life was really all about. But he had the feeling that some of those pleasures might have to be sluffed off and he wasn't sure he was ready to give them up.

Mrs. Randolph and Clay had left the room as these thoughts had been going through Eric's mind. Now Clay reentered and asked if he was ready for supper. Eric followed his friend but his thoughts were still on the remarkable change in Linn, and Mrs. Randolph, and now Clay. A little "worry" kept reasserting itself. What if they all had come in contact with something (or someone) that was the greatest thing that could happen in a person's life and he, Eric, missed out on it for himself? Maybe he should look into this. If it didn't make sense to him or seem to be what he needed, he didn't have to embrace it. After all, it was a free choice thing and Clay had never tried to push him into it.

Eric's mind was pulled back to his surroundings by someone passing a bowl of food to him. Then he realized that Clay was enthusiastically making plans about his trip to Allenville early the next morning. Clay spoke to him across the table.

"Eric, I know I have imposed on you terribly the past few weeks, but could I get you to stay by the office until I get back? You don't need to try to do any more than necessary until I get back. Just take care of any pressing matters. I hope to be back tomorrow, but if I get detained, I'll call. I promise not to be gone any longer than absolutely necessary."

Eric assured him that he was more than glad to stay, and added with a rueful laugh, "After all, it will be to my advantage for you to bring Linn back. Then I'll gain my boss back."

"I hope and pray that I will bring Linn back," said Clay seriously. "I'm afraid I used some pretty strong words when I last saw her. If she took me at my words, she may not even consent to talk to me."

"I'll be praying for you, son," said Mrs. Randolph.

After a pause Mrs. Randolph laid down her fork and spoke earnestly. "Clay, I have come to a decision. I have been praying about this for quite a while and I believe my decision is right for me, and also for you. I am going to leave shortly and do a little traveling. Then when I tire of traveling I plan to get a place of my own." When Clay tried to protest, she held up her hand and spoke decisively. "Nothing you say will change my plans. This isn't a spur-of-the-moment decision. And your marriage will have a much greater chance of succeeding if I am not here."

Clay studied his mother's face for a full moment, saw the resolve in the determined set of her jaw, and the steady look she gave him.

"Very well, Mother, if that is what you want."

There was a rustle at the other end of the table, and the sound of a chair being scraped back quickly. Everyone turned to see Arthur rising to his feet unsteadily. He stood up as straight as his bent back allowed and announced solemnly, "I will also be moving."

A gasp went around the table. Mrs. Randolph's brother, habitually inebriated, moved in a perpetual fog and seldom talked to anyone. He came and went like a tipsy wraith, and had finally come to be regarded like a piece of furniture, always there, but almost totally ignored. But he had always been a part of the family.

Clay was the first to regain his speech. "Uncle Arthur, what do you mean? Where will you go?"

Arthur steadied himself with both hands on the table edge and spoke almost haughtily, "I know when I'm not wanted, and I don't stay where I'm not wanted."

"But of course you're wanted," protested Clay. "Whatever gave you the idea that you weren't?"

Arthur blinked his bleary eyes in an obvious effort to focus them better on Clay, then spoke again resolutely. "She won't want me when she comes back!"

Mrs. Randolph thought he referred to herself and quickly answered, "Now, Arthur, you know that you will always have a home with me. And I'm sure Clay feels the same way. So you just forget about moving anywhere."

Arthur wavered on his feet a bit, then steadied himself and drew himself up proudly and announced again, "But 'she' won't want me when she comes back," with emphasis on the "she."

"Oh, you mean Linn," said Clay. "Uncle Arthur, you can rest your mind about Linn. If she comes back, she will not object to your being here. She never disliked you."

"Yes, she does dislike me. She thinks I tried to kill her, but I didn't! Really I didn't!" His face suddenly seemed to fall apart. His chin quivered, and tears began to run down his lined cheeks. He began to blubber, "I didn't go to do it, I didn't, I didn't—"

Mrs. Randolph was at Arthur's side, now. With her arm around his shoulder, she spoke soothingly, "Of course, you didn't do anything to harm Linn. Everyone knows that. Now come, let me take you to your room and you lie down a bit. You're just upset—"

But Clay had risen to his feet as a sudden suspicion began to dawn in his brain. "Mother not so quick. I think Arthur knows what he is talking about. Uncle Arthur, I think you and I have something to discuss. Let's go into my office where we can be alone."

Arthur disengaged himself from his sister's encircling arm, squared his shoulders the best he could on unsteady legs and marched forward to the study with the air of one going to the scaffold.

As Linn neared the cafe, she felt a slight tremor of trepidation start in the pit of her stomach, but she threw back her shoulders and breathed a quick prayer before she went in to meet with Clay's lawyer. She quickened her step and was soon opening the door to the cafe. Two customers were sitting at the counter and an older couple was in a booth near the front. Her eyes swung to the remaining customer, sitting with his back to her, in another booth. Could that be the lawyer? He was dressed like a businessman so it was a good chance, she surmised. She took two slow steps toward the booth when the man turned in the seat and then rose quickly to meet her. It was Clay!

Linn's face drained of all color. With a small involuntary gasp, she turned and ran from the cafe. As she fled quickly down the sidewalk, Linn told herself that she was acting like a dunce but her feet involuntarily carried her swiftly away from the one thing she had not prepared for—Clay. She just could not bear to face him and his scorn. Why had he come? Had he not said he never wanted to set his eyes on her again? Then why had he come? She really should go back, but fear that she could not handle a confrontation with Clay with dignity kept her feet flying.

Suddenly she realized that swift footsteps were following her, gaining on her, and then her arm was grasped by a strong hand and Clay firmly hauled her to a halt. He held her by one wrist, reached over and grasped the other wrist and swung her firmly around to face him. "Linn," he began—

But now Linn was angry and she struggled to free her arms. How dare Clay run her down and hold her prisoner this way! The temper she had, with God's help, held in abeyance, flared. Her head came up, and the eyes that met Clay's were flames of flashing green fire.

"Let me go," she said icily.

"Not until you promise to stay put so we can talk," stated Clay, breathing hard from his exertion.

Linn, looking into his face, felt a little foolish. He didn't look angry with her, and his usual arrogance was at least concealed. They were two mature adults, so surely they could conduct whatever business that needed attending to in a civilized manner.

Clay had relaxed his hold somewhat, but still held her wrists, and was regarding her with an inscrutable gaze, obviously waiting for her promise not to abscond again.

With what dignity she could muster, she said humbly, "I—I'm sorry I acted so—so dumb. I—I wasn't prepared to see you. I can't stay long as I must get back to my aunt, but if you want to talk, I am ready."

Clay gave her a long, searching look and then released her. "Could we go over to that little park?" he asked. "It would be more private than the cafe."

"That would be fine," Linn replied meekly.

Clay took her arm and they crossed the street together and walked the half block to a small grassy park with a few trees and benches scattered about. Clay guided her to one of the benches under the shade of a leafy maple tree. As Linn walked she prayed desperately for help. How could she ever go through this, she thought. Even now, as they walked together, every fiber of her being throbbed with love for Clay. The pressure of his strong, tanned hand upon her arm set her heart to racing. Then she forced her mind to calm down. She must not, for the sake of pride, let him know how she felt. After all, though she had been cast off she could keep her pride intact. With a carefully-willed composure she sat down on the bench and waited for Clay to begin the business of making their separation final.

So it was with a great deal of shock that she heard the first words he spoke, "Linn, can you ever forgive me for the agony I have put you through?" Her eyes widened with shock. He rushed on, "My mother told me everything she and Bonnie plotted and perpetrated against you. I will never know how I could have been so stupid as not to have seen what was going on. I have gone through living hell trying to find you, Linn. I want you to go home with me. If you come back to me, I promise never to doubt you again!"

Incredulity left Linn completely speechless. Clay reached for her hands, and when she remained speechless he said imploringly, "You will forgive me, Linn?' His voice was laden with remorse. "Honey, I promise that things will be different. I'll spend the rest of my days making up to you what we did to you. Will you come back to me, Linn?"

At last Linn found her voice, "I can't go back to that house, Clay. I'm sorry."

Clay said urgently, "You don't have to go back to Grey Oaks if you don't want to. We'll live somewhere else. But I love you and want you for my wife. Will you forgive me, Linn?"

Linn felt as if she were drifting in a dreamworld of un-reality. This could not be happening. Just last night she had finally relinquished Clay in her heart and now he wanted her back! Things were just happening too fast. She must go slow. She must know that this was "for real"; that Clay no longer cared for Bonnie. Her heart twisted in pain at the thought but she must be sure of Clay's love and where his loyalty lay.

"What of Bonnie, Clay?"

"Linn, I realized, even before I found out the truth about Bonnie, that I could never marry her. I was fond of her, until I found out about her deceit, but I never loved her. I told her that I could not marry her shortly after I sent you away. That is partly what hastened the climax to the whole mess. I'll tell you all about it later. It is you that I love, Linn, and it has always been that way and always will be! Come back to me, and I'll prove it to you!"

Linn's heart beat wildly for joy but her cautious mind laid a restraining hand on that jubilant member. "Clay, I could never live in that house. You would have to choose between your mother and me constantly and that is too great a strain on a marriage."

"Mother has removed that obstacle herself, already. She informed me just yesterday that she was moving out for good, even if you did not come home. But she said to tell you that she is deeply sorry for her part in breaking us up, and that she will never interfere with our lives again. In fact, Mother plans on traveling for a while so I doubt that you will see your mother-in-law for some time.

"Eric is usually not there much, except when I need him there, as I have the past few weeks, so it would be just you and me, Old Uncle Arthur, and the help. Oh, by the way, Mrs. Gray came to me just as I was leaving and told me she wanted to stay if you would have her. She was humble as pie. She had no part in that plot, and of course neither did George. You always were his favorite."

Then he said softly, "You still do not have to live there, Linn, if you don't want to, but Grey Oaks is no longer a house of enemies. It is now a house of friends. How about it, Linn? Will you be my wife?" His voice was husky with emotion and when Linn looked into his eyes, she saw something there to match her own clamoring love.

Neither one could remember later who made the first move, but the next minute, Linn was in Clay's arms.

Linn was laughing and crying at the same time; Clay held her tightly, murmuring endearments. Finally they drew apart. Clay looked at Linn's tear-wet face and spoke almost reverently.

"Linn Randolph crying!"

"They are tears of joy," Linn said.

"I pray to God that I never again cause you to shed any

other kind," Clay said earnestly.

A few minutes later, Clay told Linn, "I have something to share with you that I didn't feel I could tell you before. I was fearful you would think I was faking something to win you back. Darling, when I came to the end of my rope, after weeks of fruitless searching, I finally followed the suggestion of your dear friends, the Glovers, and I met your Savior."

Linn was too stunned at first to answer and then tears filled her eyes and she quoted softly, "My cup runneth over."

"So does mine," said Clay. "Even when I grew discouraged and wondered if I would ever see you again, God was there—a constant comfort. And then I received an "assurance" that I would see you again, though I didn't know what the results would be. In fact, my whole experience with God has been very special." And Clay went on to tell her in detail about it.

"Linn," he said gravely, "this whole affair has been a traumatic experience for all of us, but through it all you and I and Mother have all come to know the Savior. And I feel Eric is on the edge of coming in."

You didn't tell me your mother accepted the Lord," exclaimed Linn. "How wonderful! How did it come about?"

"Mother had been exposed to Christianity when she was very young," explained Clay, "but she left church and drifted. But when you came back, Linn, and Mother saw God in your life, it was like a confrontation with God himself. She tried to get away from Him but there He was, every way she turned, mirrored in your face and actions. It tore her to ribbons. That, coupled with being forced by Bonnie to help her frame you again, was the primary reason for her heart attack. When she realized she had almost died without God, she had a showdown with Bonnie, and told me the whole sordid story.

"Bonnie had a note for a large sum that she swore my father owed her father. She threatened Mother that she would ruin us financially if Mother didn't go along with her. There was such a note, but it had been repaid long ago, but Mother didn't know this. The first time, Mother disliked you and wanted to help Bonnie with her plots against you, but the second time she was forced into it, and her guilt of it all nearly killed her. You were directly responsible for Mother becoming a Christian."

"I'm glad," said Linn humbly.

Then Linn told about her life since she had been with her aunt. She ended it with the revelation that Penny was really her own little sister.

"We told Penny this morning and it didn't seem to bother her a bit that she hadn't been told before, she was so delighted to have a big sister. We loved each other from the start, anyway. And Clay, you will be amazed. She looks almost just like me. Just a younger version. You'll love her—and aunt Kate, too."

A shadow passed over Linn's face. "Clay, I want so badly to go back with you, but I can't leave Aunt Kate and Penny." She looked bewildered.

Clay said instantly, "We'll take them home with us, when your aunt is well enough to go. Later, if your aunt doesn't want to live with us we'll build them a house nearby. But until your aunt is able to travel, you can stay right here. But we can move her by plane so she could probably be ready to travel soon. My plane is too small but I'll rent one."

"I hope Aunt Kate will consent to go," said Linn. "She is very proud. She has had a struggle providing for herself and Penny but she has never asked for help from anyone. In fact, she would not have let me help if she had not felt I was a direct answer to prayer."

Suddenly Linn looked at her watch. "It is getting very late and they will be worried about me."

"Just a moment," said Clay. He drew a small jewelry box from his jacket pocket. He opened the box and drew out a ring and set the box on the bench. Lifting her left hand, he held it for a moment between strong fingers and spoke reverently. "I believe these belong to you, Mrs. Clay Randolph." He placed the wedding band in place, then stooped to slip the star sapphire from its velvet setting. As he slipped it on her finger, it flashed in the sun.

With a catch in her voice, Linn spoke softly. "Thank you, Mr. Clay Randolph. I had forgotten how beautiful they are. But they were never as beautiful as they are today."

"There is one more thing that I want to clear up before we go," said Clay. "I've had a talk with Uncle Arthur. Last night he was very drunk and made a confession to me. He was the one who dressed up in the long overcoat and tried to scare you into giving him that heirloom sapphire ring. He happened to overhear what we said and knew I wanted that ring back really badly. He walked along the shore and hatched up the idea. He felt he had never done anything to repay us for the years he has lived with us, so he thought getting the ring for me would atone. So he dressed up in that weird "get-up" and accosted you, demanding the ring. But he didn't know, of course, that you had already hidden it. The whole thing backfired. You were frightened and backed to the end of the dock and fell off into a boat, striking your head as you fell. He was so frightened when you lay there in the bottom of the boat and didn't move, that he ran away. He rationalized that you couldn't be too badly hurt and that someone would miss you soon, anyway, and go looking for you. So he tried to forget the whole thing by getting thoroughly drunk. Somehow, the rope must not have been tied tightly and the boat came loose and took you down the river. I thought Bonnie might have released the boat, but Mother was confident that Bonnie had nothing to do with it or she would have told her."

The unraveling of this entire mystery left Linn speechless. Clay went on.

"Anyway, when Arthur came out of his drunk the next day, you were gone, and he was too frightened to tell anyone what had happened. The boat was gone, and you were gone, so everyone presumed you had committed suicide. And Uncle Arthur let us think it."

"Poor dear Arthur!" Linn exclaimed. "His mind is nearly gone from years of drinking, so I think he is hardly responsible for his actions."

Clay agreed. "Arthur has never had a clear mind since I have known him. Wine deteriorated it long ago. He is a pitiful case.

"There is one thing I marvel about yet, Linn. God had his hand on that boat or you never would have survived those rapids down river. That is why it was hard for me to believe your story, at first. But now that I have a personal acquaintance with the Lord Jesus, I know that He continually deals in miracles."

"That is true," Linn agreed. She glanced at her watch and sprang up from the bench. "I really have to get back. Come back with me and meet Aunt Kate and Penny."

"I'm anxious to meet them," said Clay. "And we need to make some plans. Do you think your aunt is well enough to discuss moving?"

"I think so," said Linn. "If she seems to get upset, we can drop it for now, can't we?" They began to walk the couple of blocks, fingers entwined.

"Linn," Clay said, "Do you think we could get someone to stay a day or so with your aunt so we could have a little time alone to get reacquainted? We could get a room some-where. I'll tell you, Linn, it's going to be a hard thing if I have to go home without you. Do you think we could swing it?"

"I surely hope so," said Linn, her heart soaring. For a brief moment she resented the responsibility that had fallen upon her, and then she forced it away. Aunt Kate had been very near death, she knew and she did not dare do anything now that would cause a relapse, even if it meant delaying the thrill of being with Clay again.

"Let's just play it by ear," she said. "First we have to see how she takes the news that I have a husband."

Clay put his arm around her and drew her close. "Linn, I'm not sure I can go through with this. If you can't come home with me, I may not go either. I'm almost afraid to let you out of my sight. I've practically turned over Heaven and earth to find you, and now we have to talk about separation again. I can't bear the thought. Do you mind as much as I do?" he asked.

"If I told you how much I mind you might think me a love-sick newlywed," laughed Linn. "But why don't we just leave it all in God's hands and see what He will work out. Okay?"

"Since He has done such a good job so far, maybe we had," agreed Clay.

31

When they arrived at the house, Linn looked up at Clay. "It isn't very fancy, Clay. But there is a lot of love here. Let me go in first and prepare them, okay?" Clay nodded, and Linn pushed open the door and slipped inside.

Penny was curled up in the large, old chair reading a book. Kate was lying on the couch, covered with a light blanket. Kate raised herself on one elbow when Linn entered. She started to speak, but one look at Linn's face and she waited, knowing that Linn had some kind of momentous news. Her face literally glowed.

Linn stood for just a moment as if she didn't know exactly how to start and then just blurted out, "Aunt Kate, Penny, I've brought my husband home and I want you to meet him. Is it all right to bring him in right now?"

"Why, Linn, you know it is! Bring him in this instant!" Kate exclaimed.

Neither one saw the incredulity that spread across Penny's face. She had not heard a word of Linn having been married so the news was a complete shock.

Linn opened the door wide and called to Clay. As he entered the house, his eyes took in the small room in a glance: shabby cheap furniture, the floor was covered with a worn linoleum—the place spelled poverty with a capital "P." Then Linn was leading him to the slight figure that lay on the couch. Kate slowly swung her legs to the floor, with the blanket still wrapped around them, and sat up. Clay saw her shockingly thin form and pity surged in his being. There was no doubt that this woman had suffered much and he fleetingly wondered how much of her illness had been caused by a lack of proper food.

Then he realized that Linn was introducing him to her aunt.

"Aunt Kate, I want you to meet my husband, Clay Randolph."

Clay took the frail hand that was offered to him and acknowledged the introduction. Kate spoke in a low but clear, pleasant voice. "It's good to meet you, Clay. We are so happy to have you. Won't you sit down?"

Clay sat down in the rocker that Linn drew up for him. Turning to Penny, Linn said, "Penny, come over here and meet my husband."

Penny had sat as though turned to stone but now she rose and came slowly forward. She came to Linn and stood looking up at her, her face a picture of abstract woe. Her chin began to quiver and then she threw her arms around Linn's waist and wailed,

"Don't leave us, Linn. We n—need you. Please, Linn, please don't leave us, What will we d—do?" The choked words became sobs and the sobs more and more violent, as she clung to Linn.

Linn was completely taken back by the outburst and she looked first at Clay, then to Kate, who was looking thoroughly distressed.

She decided quickly what to do. Gently unclinching the clinging hands, she held Penny away from her and spoke as crisply as she could with a lump in her throat.

"Penny, let's go in the other room and have a little talk. Okay?"

Penny nodded, numbly, and allowed herself to be led into the tiny cubicle that was Penny's room. Leading her to the bed and seating her there, Linn sat down facing her. She turned Penny's face up with a gentle hand until she had to look at Linn.

"Do you really think I'm about to just go away and leave you and Aunt Kate, Penny?"

"I—I don't know," she quavered.

"Well, I'm not!" declared Linn emphatically.

Penny wiped her eyes with a balled fist and looked incredulous. "But I thought if you were married you had to g-go with your husband."

Linn laughed. "Well, that is usually the case, but in this case, we want to take you to live with us. Would you like that?"

Penny thought for a moment, and then shook her head sadly. "Mother would never go," she said practically. "She wouldn't let us impose."

Linn thought for a minute. She also had known this was a possibility but she was amazed that Penny understood her mother so well. "You would not be imposing on us, Penny. We'll just have to convince your mother of that."

"I don't know," sighed Penny. "Mother is very stubborn." Linn supressed a smile, "Why did you have to go out and get a husband?" Penny went on. "Then everything could still be lovely and all," her voice began to quaver again and tears filled her eyes.

"Penny, haven't I been able to handle things so far?" asked Linn.

Penny nodded, rather dubiously.

"Well, you just dry those tears and see what we can work out, okay?"

When Penny agreed reluctantly, Linn took her hand and they went back to join Clay and Kate.

When Linn took Penny out of the room, Clay had seized on the opportunity to speak with Kate alone. With a prayer in his heart he smiled at Kate and spoke apologetically. "I guess it is a blow to have Linn come up with a husband right out of the blue."

"Yes, I'm afraid it is. We hadn't told Penny that Linn was married. But this is also a surprise to me, though"—she hastened to add, "it is a pleasant one."

"I appreciate so much that you opened your home to Linn," said Clay. "I expect Linn told you about our problems, didn't she?"

"Yes," replied Kate.

"I plan to make up for all that we put her through, if that is possible," said Clay. He leaned toward Kate, and said bluntly, "Would you consider coming to live with us, Mrs. Marshall?"

Kate was shaking her head before he hardly got the words from his mouth. Had he spoiled everything by jumping the gun before they had gotten used to the idea of Linn having a husband, he wondered.

"We couldn't be beholden to anyone like that," Kate said. "But I thank you, just the same."

Clay tried another approach. "I expect that Linn told you that it was my mother who had a big hand in causing our problems. She never liked Linn because she was set on me marrying a childhood friend. But when Linn came back to us after being gone three years, she was no longer the same person. And it was her radiant life that finally caused my mother to come to God and also to confess what she had done. My mother is also a changed person now, and is grieved at what she did to Linn. She is determined never to interfere with our lives again. She has decided to move out of the house and travel for awhile." And when she returns she plans to get her own place.

He continued to explain to an interested listener.

"I have a very large house, and with just Linn and I rattling around in it, it is going to be very lonesome. I feel that Linn needs you to be near her. You are all the family she has. I have a very large real estate business to see to. And our home is out in the country, so it will be very lonely for Linn when I am away on business. You would be doing me and Linn a big favor if you would come home with us. If you no longer wanted to live in our home when you are well and strong again, we will build you a house near us. We need you, will you come?"

Kate had been trying to say something, but he had gone on, not letting her interrupt. Now when he stopped talking, she hesitated. He could see that she was weakening.

"Our home is an ideal place for a child," said Clay persuasively. "It's surrounded by meadows and trees and space to play. We raise our own food there and Penny would have a ball gathering eggs and watching our hired man milk the cow."

Katie laughed suddenly. "I can see why you are a successful salesman. You could almost sell the White House I do believe."

Clay laughed with her, then said seriously. "But this is not just a 'selling job.' It would make Linn and me very happy if you would come to live with us. Just try it for awhile, until you are strong and well again. Then if you don't want to stay, it will be your decision."

Kate started to speak when Penny burst into the room. "Mamma," she exclaimed, "Linn wants us to live with her. Can we, please, Mamma?" She dropped down in the front of the old couch and fixed her mother with such a beseeching look that Kate burst out laughing.

"I seem to be outnumbered." she turned to Linn. "Linn, are you sure this is what you want?"

Linn went swiftly to her aunt and hugged her. "Nothing would make me happier," she declared.

"Then it's decided," said Kate. "I haven't done anything daring in years, and I do declare, I'm as excited as a kid. This is a real adventure for us, Linn. I have lived in this little house for most of my married life."

"Are you adventuresome enough to ride in my airplane?" queried Clay.

"Why not?" declared that astonishing woman. "I'll be scared to death, but if it brought you over here in one piece, I guess it will do the same for us. Won't it, Penny?"

Penny threw her arms around her mother. "We aren't going to lose Linn after all," she cried in delight. "When can we go?"

A few days later, the Randolph station wagon pulled into the drive that curved around until it ended in the four-car garage that adjoined the house. George had come in to the small Whitebird airport to pick them up. The car stopped at the beginning of the drive. Clay turned to Kate, in the back seat. "Welcome to Grey Oaks," he said warmly. Kate's cheeks were pink with excitement.

"Can I get out and see?" exclaimed Penny, who had been bouncing up and down and craning her neck trying to see everything at once.

"Hop right out, young lady, and see how you like your new home," said Clay. He climbed out and Linn stepped out beside him.

The little girl stood gazing at the huge old house for a long moment and then she turned to Linn with shining eyes, clasped her hands together, and said rapturously, "It's just like the castles in storybooks." She began to run up the long winding drive as if she could not wait for a mere vehicle to get her there.

"Welcome home, honey," said Clay softly in Linn's ear.

Linn stood very still in the circle of Clay's arm. A feeling of intense joy welled up in her bosom until she felt she could hardly contain it. She turned to Clay. "You know, when I came back here the last time the sight of Grey Oaks filled my heart with fear, but it has lost that aura, and the sight of it now seems to be welcoming me home. I'm about to burst with happiness."

"The Lord hath done great things for us, whereof we are glad," quoted Clay, reverently.

. SOA

001

22 402.—